SET A PIRATE TO CATCH A PIRATE

When his former pirate comrades marooned Alan Waite on a tiny desert island, it looked like a slow death under a hot, blistering sun. Alan's short career would be burned out before it had really begun.

But Fate is the master of irony. For in his delirious mind, Alan suddenly heard a voice. And even his aching eyes told him that the beautiful woman who had suddenly appeared before him could not be the long awaited Grim Reaper.

In fact she turned out to be the mistress of the new governor of Jamaica. And the price of Alan's rescue was to be his return to the Spanish Main under his new rival's banner as the official scourge of the corsairs—in an inferior boat with a scurvy crew!

DONALD BARR CHIDSEY has made an enviable name for himself both as a writer of excellent historical novels, including such as *Panama Passage, Captain Bashful,* and *Lord of the Isles,* and also as a writer of historical biographies, including those of Sir Walter Raleigh, Marlborough, and Bonnie Prince Charlie.

His own life has been as full of adventure as his writings. He has covered a good part of the earth in tramp steamers, pearl shell boats, and private yachts. He has lived in the South Seas, has been a newspaperman, actor, farmer, road gang foreman, mountaineer, boxer and fencer. During the war he served with the British, New Zealanders, Highlanders, the Free French, and the United States Army.

At the present time he lives quietly in Lyme, Connecticut, and seems content to confine further adventures to the pen.

MAROONED

by

DONALD BARR CHIDSEY

ACE BOOKS, INC.
23 West 47th Street, New York 36, N.Y.

MAROONED

1

MEACHUM'S EYES were dark-blue, almost purple. They were venomous and very bright. Because the black wire mat of his whiskers grew right up to them, those eyes suggested the eyes of some beast, peering, with unspeakable malevolence, out of a jungle.

He lifted the brass blunderbuss, and cocked it.

"Get out."

"Now listen, man, I tell you again I never stole that bracelet. It must've been—"

"I said *get out!*"

There was no arguing with that blunderbuss. A stumpy thick weapon, its muzzle loomed like the mouth of a cave. It wouldn't throw far, and it was anything but accurate—had no sights at all. But it was charged, as Alan Waite well knew, with half-ounce and quarter-ounce slugs of lead; a load that at this distance, the mere beam of the longboat, perhaps four feet, could tear a man's chest open, could rip all his guts out, severing his spine.

Alan sighed. He threw a leg over the thwart. He could read, and the Articles of Association had been clear enough in the matter of share-out: "If any man hide or hold away an article of value that is part of the spoil to be divided . . . he shall die."

Alan knew that somebody had put the thing into his wallet —somebody, patently, who disliked him. His conscience was clear. What hurt was the realization that he wasn't believed. He had known that he wasn't popular, but to be called a thief and a liar by *these* stinking, drooling, ignorant, foul-mouthed wretches—it was too much!

MAROONED

"And not even a knife," he muttered, hoping that it didn't sound like a plea: he would not give them the satisfaction of hearing him plead.

"So's you could cut your own throat when you begin to get good and thirsty? Oh, no! We want you to last longer than that."

The water was thigh-high, the bottom sand and small pebbles. Cursing quietly, Alan Waite started for the bow of the longboat, which nudged the shore. It was then that Alan saw what Lennie Harris did.

This man Harris was a wizened rat, who seldom opened his mouth for anything but a snarl. He was old, as pirates go: he might have been forty. His face was the color of Russian leather, and his breath smelled like low tide. Yet he must have a heart, somewhere, for as Alan passed the place where he held his oar Lennie leaned over the thwart, ostensibly to spit into the sea, actually to drop something. It made a tiny splash, a sound that Alan, thinking fast, swamped in a curse, so that none of the others heard it. When Lennie resumed his natural rowing position he looked as mean and cantankerous as ever, his eyes reptilian, his mouth a wolf trap. He leered.

Alan waded ashore, never so much as glancing at the place where the thing had fallen. A knife? He believed so. But if he were seen to stare at that spot, the thing, whatever it was, would easily be recovered, for in these parts, in the West Indies, the water was most wondrously clear, like crystal.

Ashore he turned, fists on hips, his feet spread.

"Bastards!" he called.

The boat already was making back for the pirate brig, the blades of the oars glistening in an early sun. Lennie Harris did not again glance at Alan. Meachum, seated in the sternsheets, uncocked the blunderbuss. They were tricky things, those weapons, small cannons that could be set off by a sneeze; and there would have been no use in taking chances.

"Have a good time," he called over his shoulder.

Alan did not move. He watched the longboat get smaller and smaller, and he still could see it when they hauled it inboard. Before that time, canvas began to show. The pirates didn't loiter. Already the sun was full, but Alan Waite shaded his eyes and went on watching the brig, standing still as a statue all the while.

"Bastards," he said again, with perhaps a catch in his voice now, a catch he could afford since there was nobody to hear it.

He hated that vessel and the men in it and everything that it and they represented. Yet he watched for a long while, for this, he knew, would be the last bit of life that he would ever see.

Not until the brig was a mere speck that shimmered in the heat, and Alan was sure that even with a glass his movements couldn't be made out, did he take off shoes and stockings and wade into the water to the approximate place where the longboat had been.

Feeling about with his feet, he soon found the thing that Lennie had dropped. Yes, it was a knife. It was a simple sheath knife, such as any seaman might carry, with a black walnut handle, a four-inch double-edged steel blade. It was not notably sharp, but neither was it nicked.

He thrust it behind his belt.

He waded ashore again. Grimly, he looked around.

So this was the place where he was to die!

It was not much of an island; a blob of rock and sun-scorched grass, a brown-and-yellow platter floating on the surface of the serenely blue Carribean.

It was, of course, an atoll, a coral formation, the middle of it not more than a few feet higher than the edges, so that a really large wave might wash right over it. There were no trees, not even any bushes. There was no lagoon, no outside reef to break the sea, which slammed upon the beach, to spit up and to hiss wearily back. Here was a place unspeakably desolate. There was nothing to indicate that any other man—or indeed any animal—had ever set foot upon it. No gulls flew overhead. No fishes jumped.

Alan walked clear around the island, keeping to the shore. He might as well have walked across the middle, for it was the same everywhere—soft rock, sand, rubble. The only vegetation was grass, a juiceless, colorless, tan grass, bent, beaten by the wind; and there was precious little even of that.

The island was roughly round, about half a mile across. From the slight rise in the middle Alan could see not only every part of the island but the sea surrounding it. The brig *Adele*, of malodorous memory, was out of sight now, and there was no sail.

He knew that the sun would be his greatest enemy. His hat was wide-brimmed, and heavy, and though his head sweated he never even thought of removing that hat. He examined his lower legs. Without shoes and stockings, they had already started to show pink. He put stockings and shoes back on.

He must, he told himself, never cease to go around this island, peering. He would make that a daily habit. He must not depend upon a look from the center, the top. Every day he should encircle this island many times, walking along the shore, earnestly scanning the sea. That would hurt his eyes, but he'd do it.

He regarded the rocks and the sand. These were dull. The sand would make a good abrasive—but, to abrade what? The stones were soft, chalky, no touch of flint. He couldn't find a chunk hard enough to give him any hope of using it with his knife for a spark. The stuff underfoot was cretaceous, and it crumbled at the push of a thumb.

Had Alan Waite been a religious man he could have prayed. Prayer comforts some; it meant nothing to Alan.

He walked on, musing.

He waded into the shallows, paddling, stooped far over. He sought mussels, cockles, shrimp, anything. He found none.

He went to the middle of the island, a pitiable spot. There he unwove a part of the bottom of his shirt, saving the threads in a small hollow of rocks where they wouldn't be blown away. He tore out some grass, and put this too in the enclosure, weighting it with stones.

If he *did* manage to make a spark he wished to be prepared with tinder.

Already tired, he went back to the shallows.

He scooped up some seaweed and carried this to the center of the island, where he laid it out in the sun. Conceivably, when dry, it might serve as fuel. Could he eat it?

He was thirsty even now. Thirst rather than hunger, he reflected, would be his torture. Meanwhile he must think of staying alive.

There was no scrap of shade. This was the harshest of all. Could he make some? He studied the grasses, feeling a bit giddy as he did so.

9

MAROONED

He took off his clothes and walked into the water, hoping to soak some of it through his skin. It gave him no relief; and indeed, it made matters worse, for when the salt water dried it left his skin itchy, so that he was forever twisting this way and that, and scratching himself.

Could it be that Lennie Harris had been kinder, even, than he seemed? Could Lennie have been offering him the shorter way?

He took the knife from behind his belt, and gazed at it in amazement, as though he had never before seen such a thing.

Cut his throat?

But Meachum would have loved that.

He put the knife back.

It was imperative that he *think*, not just moon. He must *do* something.

He made another stooped-over search of the island, peering low, his aim being to find the nearest thing to a flint stone available.

What he did find, after a long while, hardly suggested fire. But he took it to the middle of the island, where the fluffy pile of shirt-threads was, and chipped at it, doggedly, with the knife. Nothing happened.

Why he wanted a fire anyway he didn't know. Instinct?. He had nothing to cook, and he was altogether too hot already. Yet there was a thousand-to-one possibility that some blown-out-of-course vessel might pass this marine flyspeck, and if that happened he wished to send up smoke as a signal of distress. Yes, that was the reason. That and the fact that if he didn't do *something* he'd go mad.

Madness, under this killing sun, was a real threat. To get his mind off it he made himself sing.

MAROONED

"I spied the ships of France as I sailed, as I sailed.
I spied the ships of France as I sailed.
I spied the ships of France,
To them I did advance,
And took them all by chance, as I sailed."

Though he struck never a spark, at the end of twenty-odd tries his hands were so slippery with sweat that he could hardly hold stone and knife, so he stopped. After all, he told himself, the most important thing, immediately, was shade. It was near noon by now, and the heat was terrific. If he didn't get out of that sun somehow, he told himself, he might not even last through this first day.

He cut some of the tallest grass, and the leaves of this he plaited into a sort of mat, a square of thatch. It was flimsy, it was clumsy, but it was better than no awning at all. He dug a hole, with his hands and the knife, in the very center and top of the island. Into this burrowed-out place, which was about the size and shape of a grave, he gingerly lowered himself. He fixed his mat over the opening, weighting it with stones. Then he stretched out to get some sleep.

When he awoke—and he couldn't have slept long—it was with a small dry squeal of pain. He jumped. He felt as though the door of a fiery furnace had been thrown open before his face. And in truth something like that *had* happened, for his awning had been whisked away, so that the blasting furious sun found him again.

He sprang out of the hole. It could only have happened a moment ago. Yes, there was the mat now, rolling like a hoop, borne on the breeze, making for shore. He ran after it.

The mat reached the sea first, and at a touch of water it crimped and crumbled, becoming smaller, soggy. He laid it

11

MAROONED

on the beach, out of reach of the waves, where the sun would dry it. He doubted that it would be any good again. No matter. He could make another; he had plenty of time. Or perhaps what was left of his shirt would do the job.

Then he went for another walk, this time in the water. He waded and paddled his way clear around the island, lifting stones, poking under rocks, sticking his knife and his fingers everywhere. The only thing he found was some sticky, dark green, glutinous seaweed, of which he tore out a huge hank. He could not bring himself to try to eat this just yet, for he was sure it would make him sick. Instead he placed it upon a flat rock well above the high-water line.

When it was dry it might be somewhat less loathesome.

Sleep would be fitful at best, he reckoned, for each time he lay down might be the last time, a thought that was not conducive to repose. The reason he was eager to get some sleep in the daytime was because he meant to stay up all night. He could get a lot done at night, when it would be cool, or at least not intolerably hot. And, more telling, there was always the chance of a turtle. He supposed it wasn't a *big* chance, but why miss anything?

The sea turtles in that part of the world, as he knew from his roving, were amazingly large. Some of them weighed well over a ton. And virtually all of that was meat. Such a catch would keep a man alive for two weeks, maybe. The carapace too would come in handy, and perhaps he could even find some use for the intestines and the bones.

Alan Waite had heard that the female turtles go up on land, preferably some remote sandy beach, at night, to lay and to bury their eggs. And if one should come here he didn't want to miss it.

He took another long, circular, complete look at the hori-

zon. There was nothing. There was not likely ever to be anything, but he meant to keep looking.

He went back to his hole. The Aerie, he had christened it.

No turtle came that night, though he kept a careful
watch. Neither was there a ship, or anything else. When he
turned in, a little before dawn, he did not rig his shirt across
the opening of the hole, for the sun itself, he was sure, would
wake him.

What did wake him, as it happened, was a sting in the left
hand. He sat up, gasping. An insect? He had seen nothing like
that, and, God knows, he'd looked! If there were insects on
this island he wished to know about it. He'd eat them. He'd
eat ants, anything.

Then something stung his right cheek, and something else
his shoulder.

Rain!

He bolted out of the hole, flinging off his clothes. Naked,
he rolled on the ground, sopping up as much moisture as he
could, luxuriating in wetness.

The shower was brief, but it was gloriously heavy. Twice
Alan Waite squeezed his clothes out, catching the water in an
eagerly uplifted mouth. And afterward he would roll again,
feeling the delicious rain against his skin.

He had been refreshed, yet still he felt tired. When he
made a tour of the island afterward, in the pearly smear of
dawn, it was with feet that staggered, legs that lurched.

He tried to make himself sing once more:

> *"I'd ninety bars of gold as I sailed, as I sailed.*
> *I'd ninety bars of gold as I sailed. . . ."*

But his voice was a cracked wheeze, and his throat hurt,

and soon he decided to save his spit, such as it was.

He got a little more drinking water from puddles on hollow rocks—puddles he gulped before the sun could. It made him realize that he should have provided against a shower by gathering all such shells and saucerlike rocks in advance, and putting them face-up in some spot where they wouldn't be blown over. He did this now. He took a long fumble at it, for he was dizzy and weak. Three or four times while leaning over he suddenly found himself on hands and knees, without knowing how he had got there. And when he shook his head, striving to clear it, it only made matters worse. It was as if he was drunk, and there was nothing to hold on to.

It was a very long and terrible day. Restless, he was in and out of the Aerie many times, and again and again his throbbing hot eyes gleaned the sea in vain. The thud of surf seemed louder than it had been the previous day, though the sky stayed clear. Sometimes the island itself appeared to rock and wobble under his feet, as though it was no more than a raft.

In the middle of the afternoon, his stomach squirming in pain, he tried to eat some of the dried-out seaweed. Instantly he wished that he hadn't. It stung. Choking, gagging, his eyes filled with tears, he fell full-length, and the seaweed blessedly came up, though it brought with it a great deal of oily, sour-smelling saliva. Helpless, his body jerking, he retched.

"What a way to finish," he mumbled, when at last he was strong enough to crawl back to the Aerie.

The night was somewhat better, though blurred. He was in and out of the hole, and he staggered around the island many times, looking for a turtle. It was as though he didn't dare to stand still.

He knew that he was close to death. Each time he tottered

14

back into the hole in the ground he was struck again with its likeness to a grave. Each time, he thought, might be the last. Did you know it when you died? Did it hurt? Or could it happen while you were asleep? He didn't care, now.

When once again the sun struck his face he knew that he was still alive, if only just; and he was cursing even before he opened his rheum-stuck eyes. He assumed that his shirt had blown away, and in that case he must go after it—or be fried alive. He ached all over. His ears rang.

He looked up.

Delirium? He hoped not. He *could* be dead, after all.

This woman who stood looking down at him wore buff *crepe de chine* with variegated flowers over a blue silk hooped petticoat, the open skirt pinked at the edges. There was Valenciennes—real Valenciennes lace—at her cuffs and along the sides of a breathlessly low neckline. There was a square smart cocked hat, ostrich plumes in it, on her head. There was a double row of pearls around a creamy, solid, but by no means fat, neck. Her hair was a dark reddish-brown, and her eyes, enormous, were green. Diamonds gleamed from the rings on her fingers. There was the thinnest imaginable sheen of sweat on her upper lip, which was delicate.

She lifted a gold lorgnette or quizzing-glass, as though she couldn't believe what she saw.

2

ALAN WAITE had never known his parents, and the aunt and uncle who brought him up, until he ran away to sea at twelve, lived in one of the meaner streets of London. Alan's education had been primarily practical. He could read and write, and he spoke well enough, but nobody ever called him polished. However, he did have a high sense of the dramatic.

Now he scrambled out of his hole, aching bones and all. He made an impeccable bow, his hat over his heart.

"Ma'am, I don't know your name, but *do* angels have names? For you must be an angel, since you just lifted me out of Hell. Ma'am, my thanks."

Straightening, he was jolted by her nearness. She was tall, and there was something queenly and at the same time feline about the way she stood. The tropical sun is notoriously hard on female complexions, but in this case, except for the film of moisture on the upper lip, there was no evidence of its inroads. The lady's face and breast, in truth, were radiant. There was a great deal of the breast visible, so that Alan, though a tolerably tough young man, and no stranger to lechery, felt his face go hot. The green, direct eyes were thoughtful, appraising, and there was no expression on the small red mouth.

Suddenly she smiled. It was a warm, full smile, but it disappeared as quickly as it had come, leaving that classical face thoughtful once more. The effect was as though she had abruptly opened and just as abruptly closed again a brilliant parasol or sunshade.

"My name is Nora Lofts," she said in a voice that was like cool clear water purling over stones in a brook. "And you must forgive me if I look surprised. It isn't every day that you stumble across a man asleep on a desert island. Especially such a handsome man."

This was spoken without a trace of flirtation. She wasn't playing the minx, simply stating a fact; a fact which, it would seem, she took to be relevant to the present situation.

She extended her hand, palm down.

Now Alan Waite had never kissed a woman's hand, and indeed he had not often witnessed this salutation, even from afar. Yet he did not hesitate. He dropped into another low bow, and he seized the hand eagerly, yet reverently, as though being granted a great favor. He kissed it with fervency, with warmth, though briefly.

"I've found one," she called unexpectedly. "Oh, decidedly! Here's your gentleman, gentlemen."

She was addressing somebody over Alan's shoulder. He turned.

A brig, much larger than the *Adele*, was standing off, with only her topsails and jibs set. On the beach below were three men. One of these was a very dark, almost black Negro, who sat on the bow of a small, trim white Moses-boat drawn well up on the sand. He was grinning from ear to ear, his teeth white. The other two were fashion plates, tall, erect, polychromatic. They wore perukes, and carried their hats under their left arms. On the beach between them lay an oblong teakwood box with silver mountings.

In the eerie light of early dawn the scene was unbelievable, and Alan blinked twice before he consented to accept it.

"You could be of help," said the woman by his side, "if you're at all grateful for being rescued?"

He bowed yet again, in part to hide his embarrassment, for he feared that he had been gawking like a dolt.

"Your servant, Ma'am," he murmured.

17

MAROONED

He had learned at least this much: if you want to seem genteel, keep your voice down. Only the *real* aristocrats could afford to screech.

She took his arm.

"Come along," she said.

Seen up close, the men on the beach were quite as fantastic as they had shown from above.

The Negro went right on grinning, as though to find a ragged man in a place like this was the most amusing thing in the world. An idiot, Alan reflected. Or perhaps a deaf-mute. Or both.

Colonel Swartout and Mr. Cunningham-Graham, on the other hand, were vibrantly alive and alert.

The colonel might have been in his middle forties. He was indeed swart, his upper cheeks crisscrossed with dark-red short veins, purpling at the ends. His eyebrows were busy and black, almost meeting in the middle. He was angry, but not apoplectic about it. He was nobody's fool. The dark eyes, for all the anger in them, were shrewd.

Cunningham-Graham was afraid, and he was determined that his fear should not show: this was Alan's immediate diagnosis. Cunningham-Graham was a much younger man, scarcely turned twenty. He was dapper, in a salmon-colored silk drugget coat with a silver brocade waistcoat and ivory small clothes. His peruke was huge, and the silver buckles on his shoes gleamed in the rising sun. Yet if something of a dandy, this man was well built, solid, not soft.

"I still say it's irregular," he protested, scarcely paying attention to Alan.

"But not unprecedented," returned the colonel. Then to Alan: "You *are* a gentleman, I take it?"

Alan smiled a little, and waved a deprecating hand. He knew no reason to put the lie into words.

"He doesn't look like one to me," said Cunningham-Graham.

Alan Waite smiled again. "This is scarcely a place in which to make a proper toilet," he pointed out.

"How'd you ever get here, anyway?" demanded Colonel Swartout.

"Some friends, who didn't like me," said Alan, "left me here."

"To die?"

"What else?"

"I see. Well, as long as you're of gentle blood, that means you can act in an affair of honor, eh?"

"Here?"

"You wouldn't want us to fight on the vessel, now would you? That's hired by the crown, to take me to Jamaica. It's English territory, just as much as any part of Whitehall itself. But *this*—" He stamped his foot. "Well, I don't know what this is, do you?"

"No, I don't," Alan admitted. "I don't suppose it belongs to anyone, or even has a name."

"So much the better."

"But if you were to wait until you got to Jamaica—"

The colonel cut in on this, a suggestion Cunningham-Graham himself must previously have made.

"It wouldn't look good for the colony's new lieutenant-governor to be calling a man out so early in his administration. Why, damn it, it might even be illegal!"

"Well, you have a point there."

"I still don't like it," said Cunningham-Graham. "I wouldn't have come if I hadn't understood that the longboat was to bring the ship's officers ashore as well. We ought to have witnesses."

"We've got two. How many more d'ye want?"

Alan Waite rubbed a forefinger along the side of his nose. He glanced at Nora Lofts. Such a homely name for such an exotic woman! She looked appropriately grave, but by no means nervous.

"I don't suppose I might ask the cause of the quarrel, gentlemen?"

"You can ask, but you won't be told," the colonel said promptly. "Your job is to load the pistols and see that neither man shoots before he should, that's all."

"But—" Again Alan glanced toward Nora Lofts.

The colonel brushed this away, as though it were a pesky fly. "Oh, Miss Lofts has seen men killed before. It won't trouble her."

Aside from the sentiment he voiced, there was something brutal in the colonel's manner when he said this. What most shocked Alan Waite, however, was his use of the word *Miss*. Ordinarily you only "Missed" little girls or prostitutes. All others, even though it was perfectly well known that they weren't married, were given the courtesy title of "Mistress" or, sometimes, "Missus."

But Nora Lofts seemed not to have heard.

Impatient, the colonel pointed to the box at his feet.

"So, get to work."

Alan Waite sighed. He knelt in the sand.

"All right," he said.

He opened the box.

They were beautiful guns—long, slim, perfectly balanced, perfectly matched, made of Circassian walnut and blue steel. The fittings, too, the triggers, the sights, the strikers, were blued, so that there would be no chance of sunlight glinting upon any part of them to spoil a shot. They lay side by side, sunk in blue velvet, sleek, sure, smooth. On a plate on the right side of the stock of each, where the hand would cover it when firing, as on another plate on the bottom of the lid, was the name of the maker: "van Meest, Ghent."

Also in the box were less exciting accessories—a powder flask, a chunk of lead, a mound, pincers, a rammer, scales, all the rest of it.

Alan went to work. He knew something about pistols, and there was no shake in his hands as he cut and weighted a couple of balls, measured out powder, and for wadding clipped a couple of small squares out of what remained of the bottom of his shirt.

"I'll buy you a new one," promised Colonel Swartout. "Or else—" he nodded toward Mr. Cunningham-Graham "—he will."

Nora Lofts had prudently withdrawn from the line of fire, and she sat, utterly serene, on a flat chunk of coral, quite as though this was an everyday occurence. A woman to be watched, Alan Waite decided. She had lovely long legs, which now she stretched out before her. Alan spilled some powder and had to do it all over again.

Mr. Cunningham-Graham was chalk-pale, and he stood very still, only his lips working. Those lips were not forming words, Alan decided. Cunningham-Graham wasn't praying, or cursing. It was simply twitchiness; and when he realized this he stopped it by biting the soft skin of the inside of his mouth.

Colonel Swartout stood a few feet off, not facing Cunningham-Graham or in any way acknowledging his existence. The colonel had taken off wig and coat, so that there would be no pomatum to infect the wound if he was hit in the head, no lace at the cuff to catch a corner of his eye as he raised his weapon. He was as bald as an egg, while with evident approval he watched Alan work.

Since these two were not actually on the field of honor they could not look at one another. They would only do that when the pistols were pointed.

They're more ceremonious about it than the boys aboard the *Adele* would be, was Alan's thought, but it comes to the same thing.

He rose, satisfied, holding a pistol in each hand, by the barrel. The pistols were not cocked.

He put one into Mr. Cunningham-Graham's right hand.

"You will hold it there, muzzle down, until the signal to shoot. Unless," he added, "you are left-handed?"

The young man wetted his lips, which immediately started to tremble again.

"No," he whispered.

Alan studied him suspiciously, not liking him. Colonel Swartout, of course, did not glance in that direction.

"You may cock it whenever you wish," Alan went on, "but you're not to raise it until the time has come to shoot. You understand?"

"Y-yes."

Alan had never attended an affair of honor, but he had heard about them. He was making up most of this as he went along, but neither of the principals appeared to find anything unusual about it. He wished he had another representative to confer with.

He put the second pistol into Colonel Swartout's right hand, giving him the same instructions, word for word, that he had given to Mr. Cunningham-Graham. He was very careful about this.

"Are you ready, gentlemen?"

"Yes."

"I'm ready."

Touching them only on the shoulders, as tenderly as if they were pieces of priceless porcelain, he placed them back-to-back. The beach at this point was level, and it was not cluttered with stones, nor was it marked by holes.

Alan stepped away.

"I shall count to five. At each figure I count off, each of you must take a step forward. It may be a long step or a short one, but you must take it. Is that clear?"

"Yes."

"Perfectly clear."

"When I count five, and you have made that last step you must remain perfectly still, not moving in any way, except that you may cock your pistol then, if you wish. You mustn't move until I say: 'Fire!' Then you turn and fire at will. Again, is that clear, gentlemen?"

"Oh, yes. It—It's clear."

"I'm ready, sir."

"Very well," said Alan Waite. "One!"

They moved apart. The colonel was clocklike, a mechanical toy; Cunningham-Graham took an uncertain step, as though he walked in darkness and could not be sure that his foot would find anything to come down on.

"Two!"

Alan felt sorry for young Cunningham-Graham, he guessed. At the same time he was worried about the man, who was so tightly keyed-up that he might do almost anything.

"Three!"

MAROONED

What was the cause of the quarrel? wondered Alan. The woman over there, he supposed. She looked like what the French would call a *femme fatale*. She looked as if she had a lot of secrets.

"Four!"

Here a curious thing happened. Cunningham-Graham snapped. He took the step on signal, and it was a long one, a stride. But immediately afterward, and before Alan could count again, Cunningham-Graham gave a loud sob, and turned, raising his pistol.

"Look out, colonel!"

The colonel whirled around. Cunningham-Graham fired. The explosion was loud, and the smoke, thick grayish stuff, drifted everywhere.

Colonel Swartout jerked a little at the shot, as though he had been nudged in the hip, but he did not otherwise move, except very slowly to raise his right arm.

He waited for the smoke to clear. His thumb drew back the striker, which made a startlingly loud sound when it clicked into cock.

Cunningham-Graham never stirred. Whether this was because he was overcome with shame, or whether, like a rabbit before a snake, he was fascinated by the colonel's pistol, nobody, Alan Waite realized in that instant, ever would know.

It didn't matter.

The colonel fired. Cunningham-Graham went right over backward as though he'd been hit with a club. He even seemed to jump backward. He landed with a thud, and lay still.

There was no need for a surgeon to pronounce him dead. Any layman could do that. His whole chest had been shattered. No man could possibly live half a minute with a wound like that.

"Whippersnapper," muttered Colonel Swartout, and put a hand to his left hip. He tried to take a step and collapsed.

3

THE COLONEL's bedsheets were immaculate, and a Chinese silk nightrail trimmed with lace looked absurdly out of place across his muscular, hairy chest. Scowling, propped by pillows, he waggled a forefinger.

"Turnabout's fair play, eh? If I hadn't made the sailing-master go out of his course to raise that island so's I could shoot a youngster for trying to get a feel of Miss Lofts' arse here, you would never have been rescued. Chances of anybody else touched that spot might have been one in a million, eh?"

"That's right."

"On the other hand, if you hadn't yelled when that rogue jumped the signal he would have got me in the middle of the back, eh? As a soldier I'd hate to be shot there."

"Actually the bottom of your spine, sir."

"Yes."

"You were facing him sideways when he fired, because you were turning. That's why it glanced off your hip."

"Yes. Oh, yes. So we're even, eh? And I won't ask you how you happened to be on that crumble-speck all by yourself. It's a piratical punishment, I've heard, and one of the things I am being sent out for is to put down piracy in all its forms in these waters. But there's no need to start right away, is there?"

Alan said nothing.

"That's right," said the colonel. He laughed, his Adam's apple corking up and down. "Keep your mouth closed and you won't have to worry about having your neck made longer, eh? Nora, fetch me some brandy."

For she went with this cabin, his possession, and made no

bones about it, fussing like any housewife, getting out or putting away her own articles of clothing, rearranging her cosmetics, her bottles of toilet water.

Not that the cabin was not large enough for two. It was in fact the largest Alan Waite ever had seen, extending the whole beam of the brig just under the poop deck. It had a balcony aft, a dazzling tangle of gilded fretwork, directly over the wake. The ceiling of this cabin was high. Moreover, the furnishings were rich.

Was Colonel Swartout, too, rich? It was clear at least that His Majesty's Government thought so, to send a mere lieutenant-governor off in such style, and already Alan had seen that Swartout ordered the captain and the sailingmaster around like cabin boys.

Jamaica, Alan knew, was an island of consequence in that part of the world, but he had hardly supposed that Whitehall was aware of this. The colonel here traveled in state, with all the accessories of luxury, up to and including his own private mistress.

What was Swartout going to do with this woman when he got there? Morals at Kingston, the capital, Alan knew, were . . . well, relaxed. Perhaps the heat had something to do with it, but certainly the same standards did not apply there as did at home. Nevertheless a doxie in Government House would be too much even for Jamaica in the year of Our Lord 1702.

Well, that was the lieutenant-governor's lookout. Alan— cleaned, shaved, fed, rested, and equipped with fresh clothes —leaned back in his chair, waiting for the colonel to come to the point.

This the colonel did soon enough.

He picked a poniard from the table by the side of his

bunk. He bared it, and proceeded to jiggle it whippily as he held it by the point between thumb and forefinger, for all the world as though he were about to throw it into the bulkhead ten feet away.

"So we'll make that a policy, eh? I mean, that we won't ask one another questions, eh?"

"An excellent idea," Alan said.

"And if anybody should ask *you* questions, when we get there—I mean, about how that whippersnapper died—why, you can testify that I fired in self-defense, eh?"

"You certainly did, sir."

"But still I shall ask you a few questions first. Such as what're you going to do when we get to Jamaica? Were you, uh, thinking of rejoining your late associates?"

"Jesus, no! Not unless it's to kill 'em."

"Good. But, you have no money?"

"None. You saw me. And I have no doubt that you had my clothes searched. Not a bob or tizzy or tester, not a moidore or maravedi, not a doubloon, an eight-piece, a toman."

"Umm . . . You seem familiar with many kinds of currency."

Alan looked out of a port.

"No matter, now," resumed the colonel. "I'll have nothing for you immediately, at administration, though I'd be glad to know that you were available, eh? But Miss Lofts here might be able to use your services when she sets up her business at Port Royal."

Alan refrained from asking what that business was. Port Royal, across the bay from Kingston, was a hell, the lowest pirate hole in all the world, as indeed all the world knew. Not Marseille nor Alexandria, not even Calicut or Canton or the notorious outlaw settlement of St. Mary's on Madagascar, nor yet any of the cities along the Barbary Coast, could compare in infamy with Port Royal, Jamaica.

The colonel still jiggled his poniard, but he swiveled his eyes toward his companion, who now sat demure, a picture of domesticity, as she put a new hem in a petticoat.

"Eh, how 'bout that, Nora?"

She nodded gravely. "I'll need a strong man," she admitted. "Sometimes the customers get nasty and have to be thrown out. I'll need somebody who can throw them out and keep them out."

"Eh? Could ye do that, Waite?"

"I could try, sir."

"All right. But mind you—" the colonel had turned back to Alan. "—You're to sell only such services as Miss Lofts demands. You are not to offer any of your own."

"I see."

"Cunningham-Graham, who was a passenger on this ship, tried that. And you saw what happened to him."

"I did indeed," Alan murmured.

Colonel Swartout touched his left hip.

"This won't keep me laid up for long. Just chipped the bone, that's all. So you'll remember that, Waite."

"Yes, sir."

"Be sure you do. I'd hate to have to do this to you—"

With a sudden motion Colonel Swartout grasped the hilt of the poniard with his other hand. Seemingly with no effort at all he bent the blade almost double. There was a *crick!* and the knife, which must have been real Toledo steel, broke into two pieces. Swarthout contemptuously tossed these on the table.

"Oh, and by the way, is your name really Waite?"

"Yes it is, sir."

MAROONED

"Odd. Well, you may go now. Nora, damn it, where's that brandy?"

The forecastle—as forecastles will, especially at the end of a long voyage—stank of sweat and tar and bilge and foul orts. Since everybody aboard ship, even the hands, jumped at the sound of Colonel Swartout's voice, Colonel Swartout's protegé was given favored treatment in the form of a hammock not far from the ladder, where the air was not quite so noisome as that of the remote corners. He declined, accepting instead the loan of a blanket, for he preferred to take his chances topside.

The night was warm, the air balmy, soporific. To be sure, he might be drenched by a shower before he had time to scamper for shelter, but this was not a notable risk for a man who so recently had been marooned, left to die.

He roamed a little, and at last selected the prow deck, a small triangle of space just aft of the bowsprit, a place where no sentry would be posted and which was not even visible from the foretop. Here he stretched out on his blanket, in the darkness beaming fatuously.

Though he was weary, all his muscles aching, he did not really believe that he would sleep much. But he gloried in the realization that he could, if he wished, doze off without any nagging fear that he might never wake up again.

Lazily he lay there, and stretched, looking up at a sky that was dotted with stars. The vessel rocked very little. Alan could hear the shush of water at her forefoot, and a susurrant rustle as it broke to run along the sides. There was no other sound that night, save that occasionally a lookout in one of the tops would call to the poop that all was well. Not that anyone expected to hear breakers or sight land or

30

another sail in these waters, but it was as well to let the officer know, every now and then, that you had not fallen asleep.

These calls might have come from another world. They had about them a dreamlike quality, an eeriness that so far from making the flesh creep soothed and smoothed the soul.

Peace!

An enormous lemon-colored moon rose languidly, with a shrug of tired graciousness, as though it thought it was doing the world a favor. Soon sequins were squandered across the sea in that direction.

Alan Waite thought, just at first, of home. Having none, never really having had one—for London could not be called a home—he often thought of this. The buffets of travel never troubled him. He could endure heat and cold, hard work, short rations, noise, dirt. He was young and he was strong, and after all he never had known much else but these. But he couldn't help hoping that somehow, somewhere, he would alight, like a spent bird, and settle down. Was there a house for him, waiting somewhere in this boisterous raucous world? A little white house in the country, he hoped, with a little white fence running around it. And dogs. And maybe even a duck pond, with a willow tree at its edge, the branches drooping into the water.

All this, for a pirate, a self-declared outcast, was nonsense. But it was enjoyable nonsense, and it made him feel good. At snatched moments like this he would fondle the thought, as a Chinese mandarin fondles his fingering-piece of jade, sheerly a sensual satisfaction, not reality.

He didn't know, he couldn't know, whether he would ever have a home. He supposed not. But of one thing, at least, he was certain: he was done with piracy. The profession of stealing at sea was not for a man of spirit. Never again would Alan "go on the account." That was a beefwit's game. Pirate vessels had to be small, as they had to be fast, for they were forever running away from something. Yet the crews must be oversized, in order to put up a show of overwhelming force, bringing about a surrender instead of the need for boarding.

This combination—small ship, large crew—made for cramped quarters that were exceptionally uncomfortable even as maritime quarters went. This situation was made the worse by reason of the fact that your mates were such filthy wretches. They were the scum of the earth, pirates. Alan Waite made no pretensions to gentility, but he did like to try to keep clean, and that was impossible aboard any pirate ship.

And what did it get you? You gambled for what you thought were big stakes. But were they? You were a pariah, always in danger of being seized, of being hanged. All of the decent world, the prosperous part of the world, was against you; and you must deal only with thieves. Because you didn't dare to put into most ports, you had to hold the high seas for a long while at a stretch, so that the water went bad, the beer went flat, and fresh food became no more than a matter of memory. You had to careen the ship on some Godforsaken faraway hot island beach, or else, more often, "bootstrap it" in clear weather at sea, a perilous and backbreaking operation.

After each share-out, granted, you were comparatively rich. But how long did that last? And what did it consist of? Some coins, not many, that could conveniently be stolen or lost in gambling. And many bulky articles of jewelry or of plate you had to sell for perhaps one-twentieth of their real value. You can't wrap yourself in a precious tapestry and so keep out the cold. You can't eat silver candlesticks, pearl earrings.

MAROONED

No, piracy was not for him. Not any longer. He didn't know what he would do next, but it would be something different. What, after all, did he have to lose? His life? But a man's life meant little enough out here in the West Indies, and Alan had risked his own so often that he was callous in this regard.

This brought him around to thinking of that lovely woman who had surprised him in the Aerie. She fascinated him. Though her voice was low, and more often than not she kept her eyes downcast, she moved with the grace and all the cool assurance of a cat. It made Alan tremble even to think of her.

And when he looked up and saw her standing there, serene in the moonlight, goddess-like, for an instant he thought that he had fallen asleep and was entoiled in a dream.

But she was real. She smiled a little. She squatted by his side, and her nearness was breathtaking, for she wore no more than a filmy nightrail, her arms and shoulders being bare.

"I told him I was going to the jakes," she whispered. "He's half asleep now anyway."

Alan wetted his lips. "Are you trying to get me killed?"

"I'm testing your courage," she replied, leaning close so that he could see the nipples of her breasts. "If you're going to work for me you'll need it."

Nora Lofts stretched herself out by his side, close. She slithered an arm across his chest. Her lips were hot upon his cheek, and her breath was fragrant.

"My God," he moaned, "what if I'm too weak?"

"You won't be too weak," she whispered, and she began to hike up her nightrail. "Here. . . ."

PORT ROYAL was a sandspit extending between the sea on one side and Kingston Harbor on the other. As such it showed insubstantial, aquiver, even wobbly, as though it were no more than a raft that might at any moment be swamped. Indeed, ten-years before this time—that is, in 1692—something like that had happened, when an earthquake caused almost half of the peninsula to slide and slither into the sea, houses and taverns and rogues and all. It might have been better if the other half had gone at the same time, in Alan Waite's opinion.

He was not a stranger to Port Royal. The town could be rated as the pirates' very capital, their headquarters, their countinghouse, and their principal playground. It was a disgrace, deplored by the respectable. It was a sink of shame. Still, and despite all mutterings, it continued to glitter and glow, iridescent, polychromatic, like a rotten mackerel in the moonlight.

The atmosphere was distinctly maritime and, in fact, you were never more than a few feet from the sea itself. Its warehouses were crammed with stolen treasure, yet the town never had been sacked. This was not a case of honor among thieves, only of common sense. Once, Port Royal had been an assembling-ground for the buccaneers, but now that buccaneering was pretty well stamped out it had become a haven for their successors, the pirates. The pirates needed such a site, as they needed, too, a park for relaxation. Their presence ashore for any length of time, and in any numbers, anywhere else in the West Indies, would have been accounted a scandal, for the practice was frowned upon.

But in Port Royal anything was all right. The pirate, mean

MAROONED

though many of them were, and dirty, suggesting rats that
sniffed among garbage, at least would not, like the cuckoo,
befoul his own nest. Port Royal was not clean, and certainly
it wasn't safe, but the very fact that it existed and was toler-
ated—and right across the bay from the new, neatly laid-out,
and highly proper settlement of Kingston—was in itself a
circumstance to marvel at.

Yes, Alan knew Port Royal! It disgusted him, at the same
time fascinating him, like some slimy beast. But he couldn't
afford to let it frighten him. In Port Royal you always went
around with your fists clenched.

He knew its devious alleys, its bagnios and blindfalls, its
grog shops. Most of all he knew its inhabitants, who were
divided into two kinds: the permanent—as much as anything
in that shifty, shifting morass could be called that—and the
visitors, always raucous. The residents were of the blood-
sucking variety. There was no honest business conducted
at Port Royal. A man's very presence there argued that he
was a criminal or that he sought to become one.

The visitors were seafarers, and virtually all of them were
pirates or men somehow connected with piracy. They wanted
a market for their loot. Also, they wanted a good time. Usually they got both, and that without looking far, though they
might leave Port Royal with empty pockets, broken bones, and
a hangover. If, that is, they left at all. For it was not unusual for men to disappear, seemingly to evaporate, from
Port Royal. Most of them were illegal entrants in the first
place, so that no inquiry would be made. And it was easy
enough to leave them lying, whether alive or dead, at low
tide mark in the middle of the night, and then conveniently
forget them. Even if you were observed, nobody was likely to

35

challenge you. It was not considered healthy to ask questions at Port Royal.

But Alan never had seen the Flying Fish, which had been built since his previous visit.

Except for the warehouses, the Flying Fish was the largest building on the spit, the only two-story one. Moreover, it was generally esteemed to be the most elegant establishment of any kind on the whole island, even including the houses of certain wealthy planters, even including the Governor's mansion itself.

Now, the Flying Fish was plain enough on the outside, though trim and unexpectedly prim amid those squalid surroundings. But inside it was resplendent. Its crystal chandeliers, its rich soft rugs, its wall hangings, its plate and porcelain, most of all the exotic and erotic quality of its entertainment—these were the talk of that part of the world, and they were described in glowing terms even by persons who never had seen them.

For the Flying Fish was exclusive. Not just anybody could taste its delights, at least not upstairs, where the real fun began. Even the downstairs, the tavern, a palace paneled in teak, was hardly a romping ground for any forecastle hand. Its steaks and its cakes, its puddings and pies, especially the delicate flavor of its wines, made it known for hundreds of miles around.

The girls were not permitted in this tavern. They weren't even allowed to show themselves at windows upstairs. Their outdoor activities were limited to a single, well-chaperoned exercise walk in the cool of the evening, if there was no rain.

At an ordinary Port Royal brothel the girls stood in doorways or leaned out of low windows, leering alluringly, dis-

playing as much of their charms to the male passers as they
dared, while their pimps, hidden in shadow, watched them
with an accipitrine wariness. The bargain often was struck
right there in the street.

There was nothing so crass as that at the Flying Fish.
Jamaica itself was emphatically an English island, but Port
Royal, its sewer, was cosmopolitan. Yet even the people on the
spit gasped when they learned that for this fancy new establishment that had just been built the mysterious backers were
importing beauties from, of all places, a French island, Martinique.

These were not mulatto, like most of the local talent, but
much lighter. Extraordinary females! They washed every day,
and they used perfume. They were reported to be exquisitely
gowned. It was even said that they wore their earring while
gainfully employed. Whether or not they were slaves was
not certain but who cared? If few of them could speak as
much as a word of English, their fluency in the language of
love was famous. Some said that each one had her individual
maid, and that for the same price you could have both.

You didn't get to these houris just by means of a nod and
a nicked coin. You were made to linger in the tavern for a
little while first, where somebody unseen in the back of the
place eyed you through a peekhole. Then, in an anteroom,
amid the susurrant whisper of silks, you were examined as
to bone fides as well as cash by the bully-boy of the Flying
Fish, a strapping young Londoner who according to rumor
sometimes slept with the madame.

In other words, you were examined by Alan Waite.

He knocked. She had insisted upon this.
"Who is it?"

MAROONED

"Me."

He heard her put down the brush, with which she spent hours brushing her dark red-brown hair. He heard her glide shushingly across the bedroom. The door was unlocked.

He had seen her, by this time, in all stages of dress and undress. He had seen her with her hair magnificiently coiffed as for a ball, and with her hair tucked into a chignon for convenience, and also with her hair down her back, the way it was now. He had seen her with and without the cosmetics she loved. But never, he reflected, had he seen her looking disheveled, rumpled. Like a cat engaged in washing itself in the midst of battle, she stayed unperturbed.

He often had wondered how old she was. He wondered if she ever had been a child, a girl. That seemed improbable. As Richard the Third was said to have been born with all his teeth, so Nora Lofts must have been born with that impenetrable aura of mysteriousness, the aloofness, that disdain that kept her away and apart from all others.

He had known the ultimate intimacy with her, and many times. Yet she was a stranger. She was a shrewd businesswoman when she consented to do business herself rather than delegate it to others. She was a fiery bed fellow, in her own time, on her own terms. But she was not sociable, not one to natter on about trivialities. She spent most of her time right here in this room on the second floor, brushing her hair, making up her face, or staring silently between the slats of the jalousies at the window, watching without expression those who passed along the street below. He would never cease to admire her, Alan knew, but it was certain that he would never love her, for he could not understand her.

Meanwhile he had no complaint. Life at the Flying Fish was easy. He ate extremely well. There had been little violence, and the tapsters ordinarily could handle what there was, so that Alan Waite did not need to mix with the customers except to take their money before they went upstairs. A stipulated share of each fee was his. This had been agreed upon, for "I wouldn't want to have anything illegal, of course," Alan had said. He was wearing good clothes for the first time in his life. And if Nora was cool to him in the day, she was quite different when once the candles had been whuffed out.

"You look lovely," he murmured.

"Thank you. What is it?"

"The governor's coach is coming. You are about to be invited to have another 'cup of chocolate.' "

"Oh? Well, I'll be ready."

"You always are."

"Step in, Alan. And stop fussing."

She locked the door behind him, and for a little while she stood regarding him as though he was a manikin, a clothes-horse.

"You look well yourself," she said. "Cinnamon is a color that suits your complexion. And this wig fits much better than the other. Sword, too. My! I hope you're not tripping over it?"

He blushed. He was self-conscious about the sword, a good one, silver-hilted, expensive. It was the first he had owned, and he knew that people said that the carrying of a sword as though used to it was the mark of a gentleman born. Alan was even taking fencing lessons at a small *salle d'escrime* in Kingston, though he had not mentioned this to Nora.

He was uneasy beneath her gaze. He shifted his feet. "Hadn't you better get dressed? So's you can get undressed afterward?"

MAROONED

She only opened her eyes a little wider, and continued to survey him.

The sarcasm was hardly subtle. Nora Lofts' status in the colony of Jamaica was known to all, and whenever the huge yellow coach from Government House was seen rumbling its way toward the disreputable suburb of Port Royal, its mission was known along the route. In the box, resplendent, beaming inanely, would be that same Negro who, with Nora and Alan, had witnessed the killing of Cunningham-Graham, and whose name, unexpectedly, was Colombo. Spurning lesser structures, the coach would make its august way to the Flying Fish, where Colombo would descent, to bow before Alan Waite and to deliver his message, which was always the same: "Colonel Swartout's compliments to Miss Lofts, and would she be kind enough to join him in a cup of chocolate—right now?"

Nora, of course, would go, for the lieutenant-governor owned her as he owned the Flying Fish. It would not have been proper for Colonel Swartout to go to the Flying Fish, but the other way 'round was all right. So Nora, in all her finery, would lurch and jerk her way to Government House. Everywhere along the way she would be stared at, and estimated, sometimes hissed, more often cheered. She paid no attention to the crowds, and it was as though she did not hear the lascivious encouragement shouted at her.

She would be gone for perhaps an hour, always in the afternoon, usually just before sunset. Then, possibly after having done a little shopping, she would return to the Flying Fish, and Colombo and his magnificent equippage would take themselves back to the more sedate purlieus of the capital.

MAROONED

"Alan Waite," she said now, "I do believe that you're jealous."

It was as if she had warned him that he might be catching cold. She herself knew jealously only by name—though it was remarkable that she took care that Alan was not exposed more than might be needed to the nymphs from Martinique.

Taut, he looked out the window, through which a terrific sunlight was streaming, a sunlight broken by the slats of the blind, so that it made the floor all bars. He scowled.

"Here's Colombo now," he muttered.

"But you *are?*"

Alan said nothing.

"I only hope that our esteemed lieutenant-governor doesn't succumb to that same malady," Nora went on. "This has gone on further than I meant it to, Alan. I was only testing you, first. As I said. Well, he's suspicious. He asked me about you, last time."

"What did he say?"

"Oh, he did it in an offhand way! But I'm afraid he's been hearing tales, Alan. We must be more circumspect. Harry Swartout isn't exactly a forgiving type."

"I can believe that."

"Of course I lied to him."

"Well, I hope so!"

She gave him a perfunctory kiss, and pushed him toward the door.

"So you be careful. It's my life too, you know. Keep your ears cocked, Alan, even if you are somewhat stuffy from time to time. I'd hate to have them leave your body out on the spit at low tide. Well, run along now, and greet Colombo. Tell him I'll be right down."

41

MAROONED

She was slipping out of her kimono and reaching for her corsets as Alan closed the door, and he caught a searing glimpse of flesh, beloved skin. He gasped, tight. It almost caused him to go back. He wobbled. But there was no time now. A louder voice than his had summoned Nora Lofts.

He sighed. Oh, it was better than being a pirate. Anything was better than that. But it could be trying, this life.

A moment later, in the taproom, he was confronted by the brightly liveried Colombo, who made a bow.

"Colonel Swartout's compliments to Mr. Waite and would Mr. Waite be kind enough to join him in a cup of chocolate—right now?"

Alan swallowed.

"What was that? Say it again?"

Colombo bowed a second time. He enjoyed himself on these occasions.

"Colonel Swartout's compliments to Mr. Waite, sir, and would Mr. Waite be kind enough to join him in a cup of chocolate—right now?"

There was a step behind Alan.

"Well, I'll be," said Nora Lofts.

She was still buttoning things, tying, fastening, as she came into the taproom. She looked truly worried.

"I don't like this, Alan. I don't like it at all."

"I don't think I do either," he said.

She touched the hilt of Alan's sword.

"Let's hope you don't have to use this. Harry Swartout, from all I've been told, is the best swordsman in the whole English Army."

5

COLOMBO DID not try to go fast but even so the passenger was rudely jostled, thrown now to this side, now to that.

"Christ, I'd hate to be the governor," he muttered.

Sometimes they thudded over cobbles and sometimes they crawled across stretches of sand, but always they swayed back and forth and up and down, rattling the occupant of the coach like a pea in a pot.

The Port Royalites who lines the way were appropriately astonished; and many of them seemed to resent Alan Waite.

"They came to jeer at the whore," he reflected, "and all they get is the pimp."

The coach passed rows of rum houses, deadfalls, cribs. It passed the naval hospital. It passed many a shop run by a Lombard or pawnbroker. It passed the warehouse . . .

That was one of Tom Meachum's goals, that warehouse. Meachum never had been strong enough to assail it, but he would hope. He might join forces with some other English freebooter or even with a French privateer. The warehouse was strong, a three-story building in the very middle of Port Royal on comparatively high ground, and surrounded by a spiked wooden palisade a good twelve feet high. It had iron-bound oak doors, and windows that were little wider than musket slits. Even so, it was guarded night and day by marines.

Oh, it was a nut for the cracking! In part because of illness, in part because of interference from London, and lately in large part because of failure of the new monarch's commissions to reach Jamaica, the admiralty court for this station was years behind in its work. Even before William died and fat Anne ascended to the throne, and Colonel Swartout arrived in Kingston to tie things still tighter, that warehouse in Port Royal had been crammed with articles in dispute; rich articles, such as plate, gold coins, silks, seized from self-proclaimed privateers, or for some other reason held pending a decision on the part of the court. Today, Alan reflected as he was driven past, it must be full to the roof, a buccaneer's dream.

Alan felt awkward with the sword, which drew many a comment from the crowd, a disrespectful one. He tried to look over the heads of those who appeared at the windows on either side. He hoped that this didn't make him look haughty.

He was glad when they got out of town and started on the long rough road around the harbor. Kingston Bay was crowded with sail of all sorts. It was the headquarters, the starting place, for the convoy system. Because of the war with France and Spain, and because of the increasing activity of pirates in West Indian waters, it was London's command that no merchantman might make the run home unless it was in convoy properly escorted by a warship. Vessels did slip away from time to time, and put out to sea on their own. But if they were pounced upon their owners had no redress.

The next convoy, as Alan could see, would be a big one, perhaps the biggest on record from this port. The trouble was that there were only three English warships assigned to the Jamaica station, and what with the confused political situation and the new regime, it was not likely that these would be reinforced in the near future. They were fourth-raters.

One had been hauled up on the beach at Port Royal and unloaded and toppled for careening, to get her bottom scraped. Another lacked spars and canvas, provisions, even firewood. All three were seriously undermanned. Press gangs ranged the streets and alleys of Kingston, Port Royal, and Spanish Town every night, but the colonists knew them by sight and had a hundred dodges by means of which to evade them, or, if caught, to regain their freedom. Moreoever, the few that the press gangs did manage to bring in were more than offset by the rising rate of desertion. Nobody wanted to stay in the Navy. The merchant marine paid so much more. And the food was better too.

Port Royal—it was one of the reasons why the town was favored by pirates who sought recruits—was crammed with well-hidden deserters from the English Navy. They would stay strictly under cover until they had a chance to ship out on some escaping merchantman, or, failing that, they would go "on the account," signing articles of brotherhood with the members of a pirate band. Anything, they reasoned, rather than go back to the Royal Navy.

They ran terrible risks when they did this, for if they were recaptured the regulations concerning their case were savage as only naval regulations could be. Death by hanging was the punishment prescribed for deserters in time of war; but in fact it was seldom inflicted. A brutal, bloody, skin-slashing performance with a cat-o'-nine-tails and a series of burly quartermaster's mates at the gangway were substituted in its stead.

Sixty of what were grimly known as "the best" were enough to cripple for life a man of only moderate strength, though, as Alan Waite knew, a hundred and fifty, two hundred, even two hundred and fifty were not uncommonly dealt out to deserters who had been retaken. No man on earth could endure all of that at once without fainting, so it was customary to spread these punishments out over a series of lashings that might go on for several days, even several weeks. Nevertheless the mariners kept quitting, hiding out. At Port Royal you could hardly knock over a barrel or kick the top off a chest without coming upon one.

Alan leaned back, his body swaying with the movements of the carriage. He was glad that they were out in the country at last. It could be that he was oversensitive; but in Port Royal, when he ventured outside, he always had the feeling that men were looking at him, despising him, or perhaps pitying him.

Perhaps one reason for being thin-skinned was the fact that it was a part of his duty to take the girls of the Flying Fish out for their walks. They must not, of course, be permitted to mix with the commoners. They were much too precious for that. On the other hand, the Flying Fish itself afforded no sort of exercise yard or enclosure. So every afternoon, weather permitting, Alan Waite gathered together his fluttering, chittering, beribboned charges. He accompanied them watchfully, glowering from the rear of that familiar and colorful little procession, his fists always clenched, his eyes alert.

There might be a jape now and then issuing from the shadows of a house or a cafe, but no hands were reached out to fondle the darlings, and no indecent proposals were made —Alan saw to that. He was a good guardian, but it was hardly a part of his work that he enjoyed. He was always happy when they got back to the shop and the girls could take their clothes off again.

His unpleasant stare had been enough, on these occasions, to warn away intruders. He never had to unsheath the knife that Lennie Harris had dropped from the boat. He never had to remind the loafers that he, Alan Waite, once had served under the redoubtable, the notorious, Tom Meachum. They knew that anyway.

And now, in addition, he had the sword. He drew it, and laid it across his knees. Since there was nobody to see him, he stroked it with a loving hand. He sighed. They were coming into Kingston now, so he put the blade away.

He did not believe, as Nora did, that he might be obliged to draw it again in the very near future. Touchy, Colonel Swartout assuredly was. But he was not without a sense of dignity, and he would hardly precipitate a palace brawl over what he might think was an affront to his mistress. For after all, Swartout was to all intents and purposes the governor, not merely the lieutenant-governor, of this colony. He was the most powerful man on the island. He didn't need to stoop to shouting and stamping. He could afford never to gnash his teeth.

The political situation at Whitehall was a complicated one, and uncertain, but this much at least Alan Waite did know: King William had died a little while ago and the throne was occupied by Anne, his sister-in-law, a Stuart. Anne was fat and lazy, and not very intelligent either. Dutch William had had a mind of his own, as he had more than once demonstrated, but nobody knew what Queen Anne might do. That, Alan gathered, depended largely upon the men who surrounded her. They were all great schemers: serpentine, tortuous, Harley; Bolingbroke and Marlborough; their confederates and enemies.

From this distance, four thousand miles, with traffic demoralized by the war and by piracy, it was impossible to know which court clique would win control of the Queen, or what it would do when it did. Jamaica was hardly in the minds

47

of those men at all. But Jamaica's governorship might have been, along with sundry other local posts.

By English law all royal appointments became void when the monarch who made them died, Alan knew. All over the empire, automatically, office holders ceased to hold their offices. They didn't need to be notified of this. It was taken for granted. The custom, Alan supposed, was for the new monarch immediately to reappoint every one of them, picking favorites, replacing those he didn't like, later. This had not been done in the case of Jamaica. Nobody in government circles knew where he stood. Nobody, that is, excepting Harry Swartout.

It had been expected that Colonel Swartout's vessel would bring fresh commissions for Governor Thomas Handasyde and others, so that the machinery of colonial government could operate again. But Swartout swore that he had never seen these. Moreover, he said, neither had the late Mr. Cunningham-Graham, who himself had been appointed to a minor post. Colonel Swartout might have been lying, but how was anybody to prove it? Meanwhile, *his* commission at least was in order. As a result, from the time he landed he was in complete charge of the colony, an absolute dictator. Nobody knew what he might do next. Nor was there any assurance that he would postpone things, put them off, until the arrival of the next ship.

This was the man who had summoned Alan Waite.

The carriage was stopped, and Colombo scrambled down from the box and threw open the door, making a bow as he did so.

Alan drew a deep breath. He tightened his sword belt. He stepped out.

The dragon was not huge, iridescent, vaporous, fierce. The

dragon indeed was a flesh-colored, soft, squirmy creature, perhaps as short as your little finger, or perhaps as long as your forearm—the teredo or shipworm.

"There's our answer," Alan cried in triumph, a finger upraised. "We get 'em through *that!*

"Umm . . ." said Lieutenant-Governor Swartout.

"Do I make myself clear?"

"No."

The colonel was not belligerent; rather he was wary, watchful, monosyllabic. He never took his gaze from Alan Waite— which was disconcerting, for the colonel had eyes that stabbed like daggers. Today those eyes were not accusatory, however. Instead, they seemed to be asking questions, and probing. The colonel was not sure of himself.

There really was chocolate. This amazed Alan, who had expected either abuse or punch. Nora Lofts was not mentioned.

They sat easy, in deep wicker chairs, shaded by wisteria, waited upon by an impassive round-faced fat attendant who looked like an Ethiopian Buddha. This was in the courtyard of Government House, a place redolent of jasmine and loud with the murmur of bees.

Alan leaned forward, his elbows on his knees, and he spread his hands, palms up.

"As a landsman, sir, you just don't know the significance of this little beastie."

"That could be."

"The teredo wouldn't fill the space between two of a whale's teeth, but it can smash a ship faster than a whole school of whales on a rampage. It's bad enough in the Channel ports, in the Low Countries, but it's twenty times worse than that down in these waters. There is no protection against it. It'll go through any vessel's bottom just like a cobbler's awl being punched through leather. See?"

"Umm . . ."

"Multiply that by fifty thousand, or a hundred thousand, and what've you got? You've got a sieve."

The colonel shifted, frowning a bit.

"I still don't see what this has to do with napping pirates," he complained.

Alan nodded eagerly, and leaned back.

"Why, it's pirates that the worm hits the hardest, sir. I mean, the out-and-out pirates, the ones who don't even pretend to have any kind of letters of marque or reprisal commissions. And those are the kind you were talking about, ain't they?"

"Men like Tom Meachum, for example?" the colonel shot at him.

"Men like Tom Meachum," Alan smoothly confirmed. "*They* can't pop into just any port any time they happen to feel like it. They have to hold the high seas for a long while at a time, months maybe. And they depend upon speed. Being a pirate is a lot more than simply looking fierce. It's very often a matter of being able to run away. A pirate spends a great deal of his time running away. He has to, since every man's hand is against him. And if he has a rotten bottom he won't *get* away. There's nothing that'll slow a ship up so much. So he has to keep careening. Much more than an ordinary merchantman or a warship. His life depends upon it, not to mention his loot."

"How does he do it, then?"

"Well, there's one way they call boottopping. It's not the safest process in the world, I can tell you that. They do it right out at sea. They shift all the guns and the water and just about everything else to one side of the vessel, so that she heels way over. Then they climb out on the exposed side with their scrapers and do the quickest work they possibly can. After that, if the weather holds and no sail has been sighted, they shift everything to the other side of the vessel and they scrape that side of her, as far down as they can reach."

"I see."

"That doesn't do the thing right, of course. It doesn't get at the real bottom at all. But it's better than nothing."

"Yes. Bootopping, eh? Yes, I've heard of that."

"It's damned dangerous, I can tell you. Of course you'd never dare to do it during the hurricane season. And even when everything looks as clear as a bell, not a cloud in the sky, the sea like a millpond—even then, you never know, in this part of the world, when a freak storm won't come along and catch you in that position and send you deadeyes-under before you get a chance to let out a yell."

"What happens then?"

"What happens? Why, it's just like broaching-to. The ship simply disappears, with everything in it. Oh, the men don't waste any time when they're boottopping, I can tell you that, sir! I've seen 'em work all day and all night and all the next day, work as if the Devil himself was standing there jabbing them with one of his pitchforks, rather than stay in that position a minute longer than they have to."

The colonel sipped chocolate.

He had been, for him, discreet. When he proposed that Alan Waite take command of a schooner and go out and scour the seas for freebooters he refrained from quoting the old saw about setting a thief to catch a thief, or even the one about fighting fire with fire. This was not kindness; it was caution. He had earlier known Alan for a mettlesome lad, and strong, and today he was quick to notice the sword.

"Why don't they careen on some beach somewhere?" he asked.

"That's what they'd prefer. It stands to reason. Oh, the best thing of all would be some actual town, where they could rent a mould and cranes and shifting gear. The way it used to be at Campeachy, at Aux Cayes, at Trinidado and Samana and Petit Guaves. But there ain't any such ports left, not on this side of the world anyway. So what they do is seek out some nice quiet sloping beach on some remote island where they won't be disturbed, and they use that. But such a spot don't lie over just any old horizon. They've got to be sought out, and found, and remembered—without being marked on a chart.

"And it's got to be an island where there is plenty of water and firewood and maybe fresh fruit and certainly a hill of some kind where you can post a lookout. Because when you careen on a beach like that, without having any equipment for it, you've got to first not just shift the guns but take them out entirely! Otherwise you can't lay her over. And what happens then if somebody with a cannon or two comes along and finds you there?"

"I see. So what you propose to do is seek out some of these ideal careening beaches and watch them the way a cat watches a mousehole?"

"That's right."

"Or is it possible that you already know of a few?"

"It's possible," Alan conceded.

"I see. Excuse me a moment."

Evidently the lieutenant-governor had been signaled by the Buddha in livery, who stood at the entrance of the courtyard.

He rose, and Alan with him, out of respect for his office. The Lieutenant-governor went to the doorway, where a tall, middle-aged strikingly handsome man in peach silk had appeared. These two bowed to one another. Gravely, Alan studied the bows.

"Your servant, colonel."

"Your servant, Master Huntington."

Alan had heard of Henry Huntington, one of the wealthiest planters on the island, not an office-holder but a power. The man was angry now. He didn't see Alan.

"I've been talking to Tom Handasyde, colonel, and he tells me that he's powerless to do anything about those reports that Meachum's on the loose again."

Swartout nodded in sympathy.

"I'm afraid he is helpless right now, yes. Things are . . . well, mixed up. But we all hope that the situation will be different when the next vessel puts in from England."

"And I hope to God that that vessel has my daughter aboard her. Or else that she had sense enough not to come, when she heard about war being declared. This to me is more than getting my sugar off, colonel. You understand that, I assume?"

"I do indeed. And it is a pleasure I look forward to, Master Huntington—meeting your daughter, I mean."

"Aye, but what're you going to do about this Meachum man? That's what I want to know. Oh . . ." The planter had caught sight of Alan Waite. "I'm sorry, colonel. I didn't know you had a guest."

"As a matter of fact, sir, Captain Waite and I had been talking about that very thing—how to catch Meachum—when you arrived. The plan is to make a series of quick sharp cruises out of Kingston here, to check the most likely lurking places, so that the Navy will know how to act."

"Oh?"

"If," the colonel added, "the Navy ever does, act. But you may be sure that I'm doing everything I can, sir."

Huntington was deliberately appraising Alan Waite, and he seemed pleased with what he saw. Swartout had hesitated, but now he stepped aside, gracefully gesturing with his arms. Alan, after all, was wigged, and he wore a sword.

"This is Master Huntington, captain. This is Captain Alan Waite. We have some reason to believe, sir, that he might be the best man for the job."

They did not offer to shake hands, for they faced one another at half the width of the large court. But they did bow. It was all very correct, and it gave Alan a warm feeling inside, for it was the first time that he had ever bowed to and been bowed to by another man.

The mechanics of being genteel, he decided, were not nearly so difficult as they had been cracked up to be.

His sword didn't get in his way at all.

"Well, I'm glad to hear that something is being done," Huntington said at last. "A pirate-catcher, eh?"

"That's right, sir."

"Like, uh, like Thomas Kidd?"

"That analogy isn't exact, we'll hope," Alan said swiftly. Huntington was sorry, and showed it.

"Oh, see here now, that was stupid of me. Forgive it, captain."

"Granted, sir."

"After all, Kidd was, uh, well he was hanged last year, wasn't he?"

"He was."

There was a pause in which embarrassment swirled, but Alan was serene.

"I'll leave you together then," Huntington said at last. "Pray excuse my bad manners, captain. And excuse the intrusion, colonel."

Alan shrugged, waving negligently. They all bowed again, and then Huntington was gone.

Swartout wasted no time. He did not even sit down again, but plunged right into the details of his offer. Alan, though a sailing man, was no navigator. But he would be supplied with one who would serve both as sailingmaster and pilot, a native of these parts, a real sea artist. There would also be a master gunner.

It was at this point that Alan interrupted.

"About those guns, colonel. You say that this schooner is sixty-two feet along the keel, but you can only raise me fifteen or sixteen hands?"

"Waite, there's nothing harder to get in this part of the world than seamen. Why, the Royal Navy captains are after me night and day to see that—"

"If I brought a dozen more, would they be provisioned and paid?"

"From where?"

"You might permit me to worry about that, sir."

"All right. A dozen."

"But even with those, how could we man the guns? And there's a point I meant to ask you about: how many guns are you going to get for me?"

The colonel rubbered out his lips.

"Well, guns too are hard to find here just now. Every tub wants as many as it can get. And the warships are so loaded with 'em that it's a wonder they don't sink."

"How many?" Alan repeated.

"Well, only a couple of carronades and a bow chaser, a nine-pounder."

Alan gave a great snort.

"Good God, no! I can't take on an assignment like that!"

"Why can't you?"

"Why, it's unthinkable! It'd be like hunting for tigers with a popgun!"

Swartout was looking very hard at him now, nettled. There was no longer any gentlemanliness. Swartout was looking as he had looked that afternoon in his bunk at sea, when he fiddled with the poniard.

He was a snake, well coiled. If he wished he could strike.

"Do you realize, sir," Alan cried, "that the man you're sending me against has a crew of almost forty and that he carries two twelve-pounders, six nine-pounders, and a whole rank of fourteen-pound carronades, five on each side?"

"You seem to be singularly well informed on this subject," said Lieutenant-Governor Swartout.

Alan said nothing, and didn't even shrug.

"Listen, Waite, you should look upon this not as a possible way of making money, and not as a boyish adventure. You should look upon it as a civic duty. Surely you don't want me to get the impression that you are lacking in patriotism, now do you?"

Alan knew when he was whipped.

"No, I certainly wouldn't want anybody to think that I wasn't patriotic," he said.

"Well, that's settled then."

So Alan Waite had his first command.

6

THE SLATS had been tipped up so that the sun, as refracted
from the stones of the street, was slammed barwise across
the ceiling. Though in this tropical land there was never any
dusk—for the night came with a rush, as though somebody
had whuffed out a gigantic candle—nevertheless this late
afternoon sun surely was less harsh against the eyes than that
of midday. When it had fleered off the ceiling to be sifted
through the rest of the room there was very little dazzle left
in it.

The street outside rang with the rattle of carts, the oaths of
seamen, the cries of peddlers, and it smelled of tar and rum
and horse apples. The big bedroom upstairs at the Flying
Fish smelled but faintly of perfume and of skin, and the only
sounds there were the drowsy still-lipped whispers when
Miss Lofts and her light-of-love fell to talking again.

"So you think that Harry Swartout's really interested in
stamping out piracy? My dear, you're more naive than I'd
thought. Why, the man loves piracy. He's building a fortune
on it. Oh, not directly! That would be too much of a scandal,
even for Jamaica. But he figures that the war won't last long—
I don't know why, but I suppose he has some inside political
knowledge—and he wants to keep piracy, or the fear of it
anyway alive so that it'll still be there, as large as a bugbear,
when the war is over and so is privateering. Don't you see?"

"Not exactly. If he really doesn't want to stamp out piracy,
then why does he go to the trouble and expense of sending me
out to search for Meachum?"

"Well, in the first place, it couldn't have been much trouble.
And as far as the expense goes, he's probably charging the

colony for that, or *over*charging it, and pocketing the difference."

"Oh, I don't think he'd do that."

"You don't know him as well as I do."

"But still—"

"The real reason, of course, is because he wants to make a show. He wants to impress the skippers in port." She flicked her eyelashes languidly, indicating in a very general way the harbor. "How many vessels d'ye suppose there are out there, Alan?"

"Sixy or seventy maybe."

"And every last one of them loaded to the gunwales with a cargo that represents a whole year's work at some plantation, a whole year's investment. A cargo that's going bad, in a ship that's already getting hopelessly foul-bottomed while she rides at anchor, isn't that so?"

"I suppose it is."

"Harry Swartout is the acting governor. Not a one of those skippers can pull out of here until he gives him his ticket-of-leave. And he'll only do that at a price. Which he's getting. Once again, not directly. He works through the muster master. And there isn't anything that the real governor or the members of the council or the judges of the provincial court can do about it because they aren't officially in office at all."

"But if the commissions come through—"

"Then Swartout'll run away, don't you doubt it, my dear. He probably has his plans all made. But he also probably has some reason to know that those commissions won't come as soon as expected. He's made a deal with somebody in the government at Whitehall. He wouldn't be operating so openly if he hadn't."

MAROONED

"Hmm . . ."

"He gets it both ways. The admiral and the Royal Navy captains who get escort fees from every vessel—he makes them split that with him. Otherwise he'd see to it that they never got any supplies and that they never could hold onto a man they'd impressed or recover one who'd deserted."

Shocked, Alan got up on one elbow.

"They *pay* to be convoyed home? Now, what the hell kind of navy is that?"

"Shh, darling. You'll wake up the girls. They should be getting their siesta, their beauty sleep. They're not as rugged as their mamma."

"Speaking of them, they ought to be up by this time anyway. And I ought to be taking them for their walk."

"Now, never mind. You can let that go for once. Especially since you're going to sail tomorrow morning. They'll miss you—but not as much as I will."

With a hand on his chest she pressed him back. The hand remained there afterward, moving about with a gentle affectionate grace but with no apparent purpose, never still, as though it was not even connected with Nora Lofts at all but had a life of its own.

"I'll wager he gave you a ratty broken-down crew and not many provisions, so's you can't be gone long?"

"Well, they ain't all I'd like, but when a man gets his first command—"

"No doubt he counted on that. What I'm worried about is that he might have some way of knowing that Meachum's just outside the harbor and ready to gulp you alive. He could, you say?"

"Oh, easily."

"And so Harry Swartout could raise the general fear of

59

pirates—raising his protection prices at the same time—and also get rid of a rival."

"But I told you you were never even mentioned!"

"Which is just what worries me. Knowing that you work here, he would normally at least ask after my health, if only to be polite, now wouldn't he?"

Alan was silent. The point had been well taken.

"Or again," she went on, "he might figure that you'll run out of provisions and not be able to handle the crew he assigned to you, and so you'll go on the account, willingly or otherwise. He'd like that. One more pirate vessel to scare 'em with, and you yourself as good as doomed. Because they'd catch you up sooner or later, the way they did with Thomas Kidd. It was the same with him, you remember? He was sent out to catch priates, and he turned pirate himself. And they hanged him."

"They knighted Henry Morgan."

"Henry Morgan was lieutenant-governor and acting governor of the colony. Acting governor's don't always get what they deserve. Though, by God, Harry Swartout will, if I have anything to say about it."

"You don't really like Swartout?"

"Like him? I *hate* him!"

She spoke with such passion—which was unlike her—that he swiveled his eyes that way, though he did not otherwise move. She was frowning at the ceiling, which was unlike herself.

"If that's the case, why did you come here with him?"

"I had to. Never mind why. Just as I have to go to him right now, every time he sends Colombo for me."

"And deliver your 'chocolate.' "

"Yes. But I deliver more than that. Harry Swartout owns

this place, you know. And every time I go to Government House, even before I take off my clothes, he calls for a full accounting, right down to the last penny. Don't let that simple-soldier's-bluff-manner fool you, my love. The man's as subtle as a serpent, and twice as loathsome."

The light was lower, and so was her hand. The sounds from the street were subdued now. Alan Waite stirred, embarrassed.

"Well, I really ought to—"

"No, I need you once more, my love. Oh, yes, you can! I'll make you to! Here. . . ."

A man's first visit to Paris, a man's first look at a tropical shoreline, a man's first command at sea—these are not things to be treated lightly. They can change lives.

As he had explained to Nora, while granting that the crew, the provisions, and most certainly the cannons were not what he would have picked out himself, still and all you had to start somewhere.

The schooner was a type of vessel new to Alan Waite until he came to the islands, to which, he was told, it was peculiar. Schooners looked fast, he'd admit that, but they also looked uncomfortable and perhaps not altogether safe in a real blow. What with their sheer bows, their thick sticks, and their scanty beam, they'd pitch and roll, that was sure.

Lively Lass was possibly the leanest schooner he ever had seen, as she was the first in which he sailed. She didn't look smart: she needed paint, for one thing, and she spread not Dutch linen sewed with round needles, but dark stiff, shabby hemp, while a great deal of holystone and seawater would be called for before her pencil-cedar deck became acceptable to any but the veriest lubber. But she did look fast. And he had examined her, and knew that her bottom was clean.

61

MAROONED

The provisions at least were a change from the usual Poor John and hardtack, being all fresh fruits and meats. Water alone never would have stayed palatable in this climate, and instead of beer or wine they carried watered rum.

Alan had in his wallet a commission signed by the acting governor of Jamaica, empowering him "to set upon by force or arms and to subdue and take the men-of-war and other vessels whatsoever, as also the goods, moneys, and merchandise belonging to the King of France, his vessels and subjects, and others inhabiting within any of his countries, territories, or dominions, and such other ships, vessels, and goods as are or shall be liable to confiscation, pursuant to the treaties between us and other princes, states, and potentates." That of course included pirate craft, though except for such craft, Alan believed, Swartout, as acting governor (he wasn't, after all, a "prince" or a "state" or a "sovereign") had no right to issue such a commission. Alan meant to be very careful.

Not that it mattered much. This cockleshell, *Lively Lass*, with her ragamuffin crew and her small guns, was not likely to tackle anything more formidable than a canoe.

Alan read the commission aloud to the men, and he permitted those who could do so to read it themselves.

It was the crew that he was worried about.

They numbered thirteen, in itself an ominous figure, as they were first turned over to him. He had thought to increase them by means of a little personal enlisting among his acquaintances in Port Royal. He had thought, that is, to brace their flabbiness and allay their resentment—which he anticipated—by a leavening of local bully-boys, his own men, who could be counted upon to stand by him in the event of rebellion. This was not to be. Man after man he talked with, out on the spit, embarrassedly but firmly refused. None of them would say why. Oh, they trusted Alan all right, but they just didn't like the smell of the thing!

Seamen, as he knew, were a superstitious lot. But the truth is that Alan Waite himself didn't like the smell of the thing either. But he'd be hanged—perhaps literally—if he turned back at this stage of the proceeding.

He got only two of the local bullies to sign up. At least that broke the number of thirteen.

The articles had a familiar ring, for they were much like brotherhood-of-the-coast articles—that is, a piratical agreement. Alan as captain was to get one-and-a-half shares of everything, net. The sailingmaster, the boatswain, and the master gunner were to get one-and-a-quarter shares each. And there were the usual provisos that "if any man coward he shall be punished by death" and about extra payments for loss of a joint or of a whole limb. There was also the customary piratical no-prey-no-pay clause. The men would not like that.

After one look at those mariners who had signed aboard, his servants, he resolved never to appear on deck unless his sword hung by his side. It was a symbol, that sword. It meant that he was not a pirate. It stood for honest authority. And Alan would need all the authority he could get for this trip.

Just the same, it was with a certain hurrah that he at last sailed out of Kingston Harbor, a man with feet widespread on his own poop deck. He kept his visage stony, but his heart made a hard beating against his ribs. He wished that he could wave to the upstairs front window at the Flying Fish, and that Nora could wave back, even for an instant. But they had previously agreed that this would be perilous.

When the vessel was well outside Alan ordered her swung to the east, it being his thought to make for Morant Point and the Windward Passage rather than risk the more open seas of the Florida Channel. They weren't more than ten miles from shore when they started to coast. Even though it was his first command and he should be bold before the hands, Alan Waite was reluctant to get far from a haven.

He stood for a long while watching the shore. He would have sat on the taffrail, except that he thought he mightn't look right for a captain.

He had to keep reminding himself that he was a captain.

A strange land, that Jamaica! He wished that he knew more about it. Nora Lofts and Port Royal, Government House and Peter's Lane, and Spanish Town— these weren't Jamaica, any more than London, he supposed, was England. For instance, what was life like on one of those huge inland sugar plantations, with the threat of a slave uprising always at the back of your neck, or the horrible chance of a Maroon raid from the hills?

He raised his eyes to those dark, mysterious, and very lovely hills.

The Maroons!

Until he had come to these parts the word *maroon* meant to Alan Waite a certain kind of chestnut tree and also a certain color, a dark reddish-brown, caused by the dye made from that tree. It meant something else here in the West Indies. It was a clipping of the old Spanish word, *cimaroon*, meaning wild, untamed, so Alan had been told. The original Cimaroons were slaves who had escaped from the Spaniards in Darien or Panama—slaves who made their way into the jungle, where they killed all the male Indians they could lay hands on, retaining, however, the females. There, as elsewhere, the Cimaroons or Maroons had multiplied mightily.

They were the fiercest of the fierce, blacks who never should have been brought over. Their hatred for the white man was intense, while the white man, for his part, sought them out ruthlessly, like wild beasts. For there were no laws about the Maroons, who had not even the rights of field hands. They were to be shot whenever seen. From time to time in Jamaica the government had imported bands of Indians from the Mosquito Coast of Central America to seek them out and expose them, for to white men with their clumsy ways the Maroon was as a shadow, never really seen, though he could sting. There was talk, too, of importing bloodhounds from England.

The Maroons had always been wild. More than desperation made them ferocious. They were not the namby-pamby Eboes and Angolans, nor even, Mandingoes and Senegalese and the like. Most of the Maroons had been Dahomeans, the most warlike tribe Africa knew. Now they were nothing, beasts, that's all. But highly dangerous beasts.

There were men who averred that even when the Maroons were well back in their hills or in their swamps, while you yourself were down on the beach, you weren't safe from their spells. For the Maroons were said to practice witchcraft, putting a hex on their enemies by means of obeah, which, as far as Alan Waite could make out, was something like voodoo, only worse. He didn't know about such things, and didn't rightly care, for he was not a superstitious man. But obeah or no obeah, magic or no magic, he preferred to stay clear of the Maroons of Jamaica.

He should have had his mind on more immediate things. His first command, scarcely more than an hour out, and here he was dreaming and mooning about hills that were beautiful and demons that weren't. He almost jumped when the master gunner, Walters, touched his elbow. This was bad, for a captain should never look nervous.

"Excuse me, but maybe you'd better come forward."

Alan looked at him coldly. Walters might have been a good gunner, but he was hardly an attractive man, being small, old, wizened, sharp as a crabapple, and with rings in his ears, and a chin that strove to touch his down-hooked nose. Besides, Alan believed him to be a spy for Colonel Swartout.

"*Sir*," Alan said quietly.

"Yes, sir. I'm sorry, sir."

Alan nodded. He turned.

"Now, just where is this trouble?"

There had been a fuss at the sailing. There always was, since not many sailors go to sea willingly. Three or four had been carried aboard, as usual. Alan had not seen these men, save at a distance. He supposed that they were drunk, though it was possible too that they had been hit on the head: the Royal Navy was not the only seagoing institution that used violence in its recruitment.

Certainly Alan never had faced this brute, a giant, black-haired, black-whiskered, who stank of sweat and rum, as he glowered. Here was a tremendous thing. He stood six feet three or four in his bare feet, and must have weighed eighteen stone. His muscled arms hung low, ending in huge hair-covered hands; his neck was almost as thick as his head; his eyebrows met in a straight line over his nose.

"I've been forced!" he cried.

Alan did not deign to reply just at first, but went on staring at the man.

"So've I!" somebody behind him cried.

MAROONED

"And me!"

Alan cleared his throat.

"Whoresons, be quiet," he said.

The two in the rear—Alan never was to learn who they were—accepted this suggestion. The giant, however, shook a shaggy, Visigothic head, and he actually took a step toward Alan. This in itself could have been construed as mutiny. Maybe the man was still drunk? His eyes were bloodshot, and there was foamy saliva at the corners of his mouth. His fists were clenched.

"If you think you've been forced," Alan told him quietly, "you can complain to the muster master when we get back to Port Royal."

"They'd throw me into the Navy!"

"That's your lookout. Now get to work."

"No!"

It was incredible. The man came forward another step. His chin was low, his lips were quivering as though in prayer.

"We're going to turn back right now," he declared flatly.

Alan teetered on his heels, and fingered his stock.

"Why damn it, man, do you realize that you're addressing your captain?" he drawled.

"I realize that I said we'll turn back."

And he took another step toward Alan.

Alan lost his head then. He whipped out his sword.

Yet the giant didn't retreat. He stood, instead, looking at the point of the sword, no more than four or five inches from his chest. He did not seem angry, but neither did he show any sign of fear. Suddenly he looked up at Alan's face, and for the first time there was a real expression on his own countenance. He sneered.

MAROONED

"So we're mighty brave when we've got a steel toothpicker in our hand, huh?"

Alan did not hesitate. He had hesitated too long already. He had made a serious tactical mistake when he drew that sword, a mistake that would be held against him throughout the voyage, unless he did something to rectify it. He sheathed. He unbuckled his sword belt, and handed the sword, together with his coat and his new tricorne, to a startled Gunner Walters.

"Hold these for me, please, while I teach this man manners."

He threw himself against the giant.

There were two long gray outjutting teeth in the upper jaw. These were Alan's first targets, now right, now left fist. Blood splattered. The giant grunted, but instead of falling back he charged. Alan jumped aside.

Somebody snickered.

Alan caught the outthrust left wrist and hipped against the mariner, who stumbled and went to one knee. Alan sprang upon him, punching.

But the big one was quick. He fell, and rolled on his back, and a heavy bare foot, the heel as hard as any rock, caught Alan in the chest, causing him to stagger back.

Before Alan could come in again the giant had scrambled to his feet. The fanglike front teeth were missing and the face was splashed with gore, but Goliath was not seriously hurt. He had been bitten by a couple of pesky gnats, that was all. It had been merely enough to put an edge on his rage.

When he came in again Alan dove, catching him around the waist, hooking his legs. The two fell thuddingly. They rolled with the roll of *Lively Lass*, now this one on top, now that one, but locked in such tight embrace that neither was able to injure the other.

MAROONED

As to sheer strength, Alan knew, he was outmatched. He had started wrong. He should have kept free of this bear as much as possible, moving fast.

Blows rained upon the back of his head now, and he wriggled lower, striving to reach the giant's testacles with an elbow.

But this hulk had wrestled before. He was no stranger to rough-and-tumble. He knew what Alan was trying to do, and he met that attempt with simple effectiveness when he bit Alan on the shoulder.

Alan almost screamed, and his grip slackened so that the mariner was able to hoist him higher in an effort to lock his legs. Alan lifted his head sharply, and it clunked against the giant's chin. Alan did this again. He got an arm free—sweat was making both men slippery—and reached up, fumbling. His hand found an ear. He twisted that ear with all his strength.

Again they rolled with the schooner, and Alan's left elbow was banged upon the deck, which knocked feeling out of it for a little while. They were slammed against the foremast, and as though by spoken agreement broke apart from one another. Panting, they rose to their feet.

Alan leaned against the mast for a moment. His head sang. His hands felt huge, swollen as they were, the knuckles stinging, on fire. Sweat streamed from him. Pain jabbed at his shoulder, and pain throbbed in a dozen other places, for the giant had made telling use of elbows, feet, fists, knees.

He had to keep on fighting. He would have dropped if he hadn't.

The giant came in again.

Alan slipped outside of an arm that would have enwrapped him in murderous embrace. He found beard with his left hand, and jerked downward. With his right fist he punched the face twice, three times. The pain in that hand was almost unbearable. It shrieked.

He was on hands and knees. He didn't know how this had happened. A sneak blow on the part of the giant? More likely Alan had suffered a fainting spell, the result of that pain.

The giant was kicking him. Alan threw both arms around one of the giant's feet and jerked it forward.

Nobody interfered with this fight. As he battled back and forth, Alan Waite was aware of legs near him, and bare feet. But he never touched anybody else, and the feet and legs when he rolled toward them silently faded.

Once a fist found his testacles, and pain enveloped him like smoke. He went to his knees, and lurched forward, arms spread, eyes closed. For the next half-minute he knew nothing at all. He hung on to the giant's legs. It was all that he could do.

Then he became aware of the hand. He and the giant were clamped in a sweat-slimy embrace. They were tangling their legs, their arms were fastened. But the giant must have gained some release for one arm, for a hand began to creep up Alan's chest. Alan could not see it, that hand, but he could feel it. It was like a monstrous spider, the fingers legs, the thumb dragging. Alan drew his chin down, and tightened his throat muscles. But the hand, inching upward, scorned to reach for Alan's throat. It passed over Alan's cheek very slowly, for the elbow of this giant was pinned between the two bodies.

His eyes! The thumb would seek them, first one, then the other. Alan had once seen a man's eyes gouged out. It was extraordinarily easy, given a strong hand.

The fingers crawled a little farther, the thumb slid up.

Alan threw his head back. Instantly the spider-hand

slipped lower, feeling for the throat. With a tremendous effort Alan arched his back, pushing up especially with his right hip. He relaxed abruptly, and then arched again. The hand reached his throat, but the other hand, which had been prisoning Alan's left arm, slipped.

So that arm was free. Alan brought it up, and scrabbled until the hand found hair. This was not beard but the back of the head. It served as well. Alan pulled it sideways, wrenching it with all his might. The giant made a little squeal, which slid back into something like a sob, and he released Alan, trying to get to his feet. He kicked, but too soon. The effort, perhaps also the movement of the vessel, cost him his balance. He sat on the deck.

Opening his eyes at last, Alan blinked through a flickering crimson curtain of agony at the man who had been trying to kill him.

What was the trouble? The giant simply sat there, swaying a little. He showed very pale, and greenish at the temples, as though he was about to be sick.

Somehow Alan got to his feet. Groggily, understanding sank into him. The giant too was weak! He too had been pressed and pounded by pain until he could find no last scrap of strength anywhere in his body!

Walking carefully, lest he lurch, his legs wide apart, he went to where the giant sat. He kicked the giant once, in the left cheekbone, and the giant toppled as easily as any child's doll. Alan kicked him again, in the other cheekbone.

He stood looking down at the hulk.

"I ought to throw you overboard," he said. "But we need all hands. So stick your head into a bucket of seawater and go to work. Otherwise I really will hammer you!"

As he started for his cabin he had the impression that the

vessel was unwinding itself. Tension slacked. Men began to move about, though they were uncommonly quiet. Even, it would seem, the lookout, until now like all the others engrossed in the fight, returned to his duties. Presently there was a cry.

"Sail! Sail three points off the starboard bow."

"Get me my glass," said Alan Waite.

Soon afterward he lowered that glass and handed it back to the sailingmaster, an old slat of a man.

"Damned inattentive crew we've got here, Hake."

"Yes, sir."

"Look, she's almost on us." He pointed. "Well anyway, make right for her."

"Yes, sir."

7

THAT DILATORY sentry was right only in spirit. There is a saying at sea that a ship carrying a full press of canvas has "everything cracked on but the cook's shirt." But in the case of the vessel that they now saw so unexpectedly close at hand, not an inch of sail showed, yet there were many shirts.

She had no way on her, but wallowed like a raft. It was impossible to tell whether she was a ship, a brig, or a barkentine, for most of the spars had been stripped from her, and she had no standing rigging at all, though the body of the vessel itself seemed sound. Her gunwales were lined with men who, naked to the waist, wildly waved their shirts. Perhaps they were shouting as well: the distance was still too great to be sure of that.

Despite the signals of distress—or perhaps because of them, since a slow-sailing pirate vessel might well resort to such a lure—Alan Waite approached with great caution, using only his jibs and topsail. All his guns had been shotted and run out. Pikes and cutlasses had been distributed.

Alan would have preferred to have the other skipper come to him in his own gig or cock, but it was clear that no such boat existed, so with a sigh Alan ordered the Moses launched. For oarsman he picked that same mariner with whom he had so recently tussled, and whose name, he now learned, was Lemuel Gray. Lem had taken Alan's advice and ducked his head into a bucket of water, and though badly battered, he was walking about again. He could not seem to take his eyes from his skipper, the man who had whipped him.

Lem Gray had only the oars—splinters in his mighty hands —but Alan carried, besides his sword and knife, a couple of pistols that had been primed and shotted and thrust behind his belt. All the same, he was uneasy inside as they approached the other vessel.

He needn't have been. The distress of the brig *Wallingford*, out of London, was genuine. Her decks were in the greatest confusion. Her hatches were open, torn off, and a glance told that her hold was empty, so that she rolled loggily. Her sticks, without support, could barely stand. Her skipper and her hands, though they looked savage enough, stripped to the waist as they were, instead of attacking Alan all but kissed him, so happy were they made by his presence.

One thing at least was sure: there would be no prize money involved here, no legal loot. Had *Wallingford* been deserted, had she constituted a derelict in the eyes of the law, Alan and his disreputable mariners might have cut a pretty melon. As it was, they might be entitled to a small fee for lending *Wallingford* enough canvas and spars to jury-rig a mast and sails with, and for escorting her to Kingston in her crippled condition. But even this they would not get immediately, for there wasn't a pennypiece anywhere else on the vessel.

"Took the very rug off my cabin floor, the damned scavengers," Captain Ross cried. "Took every stick of furniture that they could move. Didn't leave a thing. Stuff they couldn't possibly have used themselves, they took that too."

"Was this Tom Meachum's gang?"

"I wouldn't know. He didn't introduce himself. And this is the first time I've ever been in these parts. It'll be the last time too, if I have anything to say about it."

The technique was familiar. But Alan was amazed to learn that pirates had been working so close in to Kingston.

"A large man with dark-blue eyes and black whiskers? Very bright eyes? And a wart on the left side of his nose?"

"That's him."

MAROONED

"Disagreeable?"

"Very."

"And the vessel was a brig?"

"She was a brig all right. I didn't get her name."

"*Bucephalus?*"

"Eh?"

"That's what she used to be called anyway. I think it was a horse; the horse of Alexander the Great. But I'm not sure of that. And anyway they might have changed the name. They like to change the name of a vessel whenever things are slow and they can't think of anything else to do. They vote on it."

Captain Ross fisted his hips, and he put his head to one side like an inquisitive bird.

"Say, mister, you seem to know a hell of a lot about those pirates. Who are you, if I may ask?"

Alan showed him his commission. Captain Ross, frowning, his lips going read every word of it.

Alan went on: "This brig—she was fast?"

"No, she was slow. That flummoxed me. I'd always heard that pirates favor speed."

"And so they do."

"Well, this one took almost all day to creep up on us, even though we're anything but fast ourselves."

When Alan Waite had been marooned, *Bucephalus* needed careening. He had assumed that they would do this work soon after they'd got rid of him, though they had not been near any of their possible careening beaches at the time. Something must have come up to deter them—some prize, or a quarrel: they were a marvelously quarrelsome pack, Tom Meachum's freebooters.

With her bottom scraped, *Bucephalus,* as Alan well knew,

could overhaul almost any vessel in these waters, and certainly would have had no trouble with this clumsy apple-cheeked *Wallingford*. It must be that they had not done this, though their very lives could depend upon it. Perhaps they were on their way to a careening beach right now? That might account for their nearness to Kingston? Now, which beach would it be? Ah, yes! Of course!

The *Wallingford's* skipper spluttered on.

"Took my periwig. Took my astrolabe. Hell, they even took my passenger."

"Passenger? What would they want a passenger for?"

"Hold her to ransom, I suppose."

"Her?"

"She's a daughter of a rich planter there in Jamaica, from what I hear, and she'd been home for schooling. They don't have schools there in Jamaica, you know?"

"I know. And what's the name of this planter?"

"Huntington. Henry Huntington. They tell me he's very rich. She certainly had gorgeous clothes. They took all of those too, besides taking her."

"Oh, Huntington."

"Know him, do you? You seem to know all sorts of people, mister?"

"I've met him."

"Now, if you could just let us have some provisions, besides that canvas you already mentioned, so's we won't have to keep signaling to you on the way to Kingston every time we get hungry—"

"I'll let you have the provisions," Alan cut in, "but I'm not going to escort you to Kingston. You can get there yourself."

"Oh? And where're you going?"

"I'm going to get that girl back," said Alan Waite.

MAROONED

There were times that day and the following night when the sailingmaster, Hake, compared his skipper with a dog on a scent, so absorbed was he, so unaware of anything else. Master Hake knew his navigation well enough. He could say the compass, keep his eye peeled on the half-hour glass in the bittacle, count the knots as they sped, wet, past the tin. He was handy with a ring-dial or a hog-yoke, and could read a rutter as well as the next pilot. But though he knew something about the stars, most emphatically he didn't fadge with sailing at night when you were anywhere near shore. It wasn't decent.

The custom, of course, save in the open sea, was to heave-to at sundown, the only safe and sensible practice. But to try to get Captain Waite to do that would be like trying to persuade a setter, when about to point, to lie down and take a nap instead. Hake only hoped that this youngster knew what he was doing.

Alan, in fact, had a plan, but it was a plan fraught with risk. For this reason if for no other he did not care to disclose it to the rest. They were not notably valorous, he suspected, these officers and hands of his. And it was clear that they never had been touched by chivalry. What Alan proposed to do called for dash as well as perfect timing. Timorousness could have no part in it. So he kept his mouth shut, except to give orders.

His motive too was plain to him, but like his methods he preferred to keep this a secret for the present. The rescue of the Huntington child from the Meachum gang would hardly go unpraised. Alan, if he could put it over, would be a hero. It was not the applause but the more material rewards of spectacular heroism that he craved, however. Huntington was rich, and surely Huntington would show his gratitude in cash form. At the very least Huntington would use his considerable influence to see that Alan Waite was properly equipped for his task.

The showiness of the deed, if he could do it, was uppermost in his mind. It must be dramatic.

The plan had appeared to him full-blown, with all details. It depended upon how long it took *Bucephalus*, overloaded as she was, and badly barnacled, to make the run from the scene of her crime the previous day, off the coast of St. Thomas-in-the-East, to a certain small island near Tiburon, the westernmost tip of Hispaniola. In this wind, if it held, Alan reckoned, she could make it in about thirty-four hours. She would arrive, then, with several hours of daylight to spare. Since a careening was always done under stress, under tension, she would immediately be hauled up on the beach—an ideal one for that purpose—and her guns taken out.

The guns, the cannons, would be on the beach itself. Several days would be needed to build platforms for them, so that they could be fired.

This island, unlike the even smaller blob of rock upon which Alan Waite had been marooned, had a name, although Alan did not know what it was. But he was thoroughly acquainted with the island itself, which might have been designed with piracy in mind. It was surrounded by a reef, but there was an excellent pass on the east side, a pass wide enough to admit any sloop or brig of piratical proportions though hardly wide enough for the accomodation of a warship. Nor was it deep enough for a warship. Warships, with all their guns, asked for a great deal of clearance.

True, there were no streams or springs on the island, only, from time to time, pools of rainwater. But there were many

MAROONED

coconut trees, and the green coconut always gives a good supply of fresh water. There was no high place for a lookout, but there was a lagoon that teemed with fish, and, best of all, there was a beach so gently sloping as almost to seem to make the backbreaking business of careening easy.

It certainly would be that island. They wished to do a real job on it this time, no doubt having relied upon boottopping too often of late; and the island was the place for that. This would account for the presence of *Bucephalus* so far south of her usual haunts in the Strait of Florida.

Nevertheless the pirates, as always, would be wary. They were men who habitually looked over their shoulders. They knew when they were vulnerable. They'd rush the job, all the while scanning the sea.

It was Alan's hope to approach El Pudendo under cover of night, and to stand off and on just outside of the pass until daylight gave him a chance to go in. Warned, Meachum's men could float their brig again and mount at least a few guns. Taken by surprise, they would be helpless.

Creeping up on a flat island that is protected by a reef was not an assignment many men would seek. The crew, understandably, were twitchy; but Alan was inexorable. He forbade them to sing, even for the purpose of keeping up their spirits. No sort of torch was to be used, nor might the cook light his stove just before dawn, as was his custom. Triple lookouts had been posted, and Alan, who was on deck almost all the time, repeatedly visited these, checking them. There must be no sleep tonight!

These lookouts, aloft and alow, were warned to keep their eyes *and* their ears open. The island might be hard to see, but an alert sentry could hear the mumble of surf on that reef.

MAROONED

The night was obliging. The stars tumbled out, neck and crop, early, but there was no moon. The wind stayed steady, just abaft the starboard beam. *Lively Lass* ran along with booms swung far out, the sea speaking loudly at her bows.

It must have been well after midnight when a lookout in the foretop—and he was quickly echoed and confirmed by the one in the main—shouted down that he thought he could hear breakers dead ahead.

In a little while they could all hear those breakers. It was a distant, hollow, *boo-oo-oom*. To a man on shore, safe in his bed, it might have seemed a pleasant sound. To a man at sea it was ominous.

Alan ordered all canvas struck excepting the jibs. The shush of water at the bows subsided. *Lively Lass* no longer was bowling along. She was barely in a glide.

The dull blurred roar got nearer and nearer.

Of course it could have been the coast of Haiti. They could have missed the tiny island. But Alan didn't think so.

He washed, humming, and changed his clothes, and in the first faint smearings of dawn he shaved. He put on his tricorne with the plume, and he buckled on his sword. He went topside again.

There it was, splashed with the pastels of early morning. And there too was *Bucephalus*, lying on her side, ashore.

They had been seen, and pirates scurried back and forth like black ants when the nest has been kicked. But Alan knew that there wasn't much they could do in the time they had.

He ordered the sailingmaster, Hake, to loiter close to the entrance of the pass. On no account, Alan said, was he to go through that pass into the lagoon. Not that there wasn't room! But Meachum's men were experts at the art of offshore piracy, the attacking of vessels in a swarm of small boats. Conceivably, before *Lively Lass* could be put about, she might be boarded and taken.

The carronades he ignored, but he checked every detail of Walters' preparation with the nine-pounder in the bow, making sure that the match tub was there, and plenty of balls, and the sponges and swabs and worms and all the rest of it. At last he nodded. The carronades threw a heavy charge, but not far. They might be fine at close quarters. They'd be useless here. But the nine-pounder could readily reach the shore. Alan ordered the master gunner to lay and aim it at *Bucephalus*, an easy target as she lay there helpless like some huge landed fish.

"Now put the Moses over."

"Ain't you going to—"

"Sir!"

"Sir, ain't you going to—"

"No."

Lem Gray himself pleaded to go as oarsman, but Alan shook his head. Alan was prepared to do this thing alone. But he did carry his sword and pistols.

The Moses was flat-sterned, flat-bottomed, light, and very fast. It was good to row, taking the kinks from his muscles. He still was sore from the fight of the previous morning, but he believed that he could handle himself.

He never turned his head. He went through the pass easily enough, combers smashing to right and left, the air all iridescent with spray, a million tiny rainbows. He came to calmer water, green here instead of the brilliant blue of outside. Even then he did not turn.

They must have been wondering, those men behind him on

the shore, those maritime rats, what was the meaning of this solo visit? Let them wonder. Let them worry.

Not until the Moses had scraped sand, and Alan had stepped fully out of it, did he face them, assembled.

He whipped off his hat and held it over his heart as he made a bow.

"So you see," he said, "I've come back."

8

PIRATES ARE a superstitious, ignorant set of men. Three of these at sight of Alan Waite screeched and ran away, terrified. And many a suntanned, wind-reddened face among those who remained went pale. Many a lip twitched. There was perspiration on most of the foreheads.

The terror of the West Indies, the malicious enemy of mankind, outlaws without truth, without regret, sunk in sin beyond retrieve, nonetheless they blanched at the sight of a single man. And why not when that man *must have been dead?*

"Well, ain't you glad to see me?"

He was careful, however, not to move. He had the lightnings playing about his feet here, and he knew it. The sea alone should be at his back. There wasn't one of these whom he'd trust, for he was familiar with their methods and knew that they never committed murder from before if they could possibly contrive to commit it from behind.

The camp was a hodgepodge. No attempt had been made to regulate or to decorate it. The run-out cannons were everywhere, with their appurtenances. The ground was littered with leather jacks, fish heads, coconut husks, chips of wood, scraps of bright clothing. The galley stove, walled with bricks, stood more or less in the center.

But there was no headquarters, as there was no stockade. The tents were scattered without arrangement. Each consisted of three or four oars or small spars fastened with cord at the top, forming a cone rather like the framework of an American Indian tepee, and covered with a tarpaulin. Tarpaulins too had been thrown over the piles of loot, which, like everything else here, had been strewn haphazardly.

MAROONED

Never before had Alan felt such a distaste for the vulgar, senseless, inefficient business of piracy.

Though there was an oaken chest containing money—and probably it was very heavy by this time—most of the loot consisted of professional or scientific instruments for which the pirates had no conceivable use but feared to throw away. There were ship's spars and other parts, and articles of clothing. For such wares, then, these scoundrels killed. And when they had them they didn't know what to do with them.

Yet they counted and recounted those things, making many a list, estimating, calculating, squabbling about every division, each keeping track of his own, ready as he was to protect it with his or somebody else's life. For all the slapdash the sundry piles suggested these pirates knew where every bit of loot was. It was because he was accused of stealing from such a pile that Alan Waite had been marooned. It meant that much to these sad, misbegotten men.

The men themselves, aside from looking scared, looked tired. They had probably been working most of the night. Each had picked up a weapon, no doubt as soon as *Lively Lass* was sighted, and they stood in a semicircle now, unsure of themselves, narrowly watching Alan.

Tom Meachum shuffled forward. It was expected of him. His eyes were spurts of vinegar, his lips were pushed out in a snarl.

"How'd you stay alive?"

"Why don't you guess?"

"Somebody took you off!"

"I swam," Alan said solemnly.

"Somebody came along and rescued you!"

Alan tossed him a toothy smile. "Have it your own way," Alan said carelessly.

He was, however, thinking fast. And he knew that he must act quickly. It lifted his heart to see those gaping faces and hear those grunts of amazement, but he couldn't afford to play his part too long. Soon the astonishment would subside, and they'd set upon him, and mash him. He'd had his moment, now to business.

"Well, I won't keep you from your work," he drawled. "I won't take long. Unless of course you want my men to knock the gizzards out of you first?"

"He jerked his head to indicate *Lively Lass*.

"There's a nine-pounder mounted in the bow, and a real gunner has her in charge. He's got a glass, that gunner. And he's watching me this very second. And he'll keep right on watching me, as long as I stay here. He has his orders. If any of you set upon me, or if I so much as draw my sword or even just lift my arm, he fires. And he goes on firing. Well, I think you know what'd happen then."

He paused, to let their imaginations encompass this. There was many a glance cast askance at the schooner.

"That won't do *you* any good," somebody cried.

Alan looked at the man.

"It won't do *you* any good either," he pointed out. "Besides, why should you want to jump on me?" Alan went on. "I've come here to do you a favor. I've come to take that Huntington brat off your hands."

He had by this time deduced that she was in a tent not twelve feet from where he stood. This was the only tent the tarpaulin of which was fully drawn, so that nothing could be seen of its interior.

Kidnapping. That's what they called it in London. It was a well-organized crime there. Gangs of kidnappers roamed the streets and picked up children who seemed to have no one to protect them. They sold these kids to ship's skippers bound for the American mainland colonies, where in turn they were sold as servants on seven-year or fourteen-year indentures.

It was a dirty enough racket, this kidnapping. But why should anybody want to practice it out here? With all the black slaves there were in Jamaica and the other islands, there was no call for small indentured white servants.

Alan sighed. He waggled his hands from the wrist, shrugging as though it was plain that he was correcting a stupid mistake on the part of the persons he talked to.

"You know you only took her on impulse. Just because you like to take everything that isn't actually nailed down. And now you're wondering what to do with her. Isn't that so? Sure, her father's rich! And you *are* interested in getting a ransom for her! But how could you ever arrange to return her? And how could you do that? Would you trust any of your number to go to Jamaica and accept the ransom money, even supposing that it was paid without the child? Oh, sure, they'd come right back with it, now wouldn't they? Oh, sure!"

He had them for the moment. They were slow thinkers, but something like this must have occurred to them, he reasoned. His own words but crystallized it in their minds.

Yet, again, he must act fast. These greedy narrow men didn't give up anything lightly, even a white elephant.

"So let's not dillydally," he said briskly. "I've got better things to do than dicker with beefwits like you. On the other hand,,I *would* like to help my friend Henry Huntington. So let's have her."

He nodded at the closed tent.

"Let's have her forth," he said. "Unless you want me to raise my arm?"

The tarpaulin was stirred from within.

MAROONED

"Does somebody want to see me?"
Helena Huntington stepped forth.
"Oh, my God," whispered Alan.

A wonderful thing is an obsession, an *idèe fixe* as the French call it. It comes from nowhere, unaccountably, and in the face of the most compelling reason it still stubbornly refuses to return there.

Nobody ever had said anything, in Alan Waite's presence, about the age of the Huntington girl. He had taken her smallness and her tender age for granted. It had never even occured to him that she might be anything but a child.

Thus it was that when he saw her in the flesh he gasped. Helena Huntington was beautiful. She was gloriously beautiful, a woman who would have turned heads in any place and at any time. She might have been twenty, twenty-one. She was tallish, thin, and had a fine carriage, a walk naturally graceful. Her features might have been those of a Greek goddess, yet they were anything but insipid. In the face she much resembled her father, whom Alan remembered as a strikingly handsome man, though what in him might have hinted at weakness fitted perfectly her own femininity. She might have been classed as a blonde, yet there was no touch of Scandanavia about her: she was as English as crumpets for breakfast. Her hair was not yellow but a very light but bright brown. Her eyes were long, a dark blue in color, curiously tiptilted at the outside corners. They didn't look their best just now, those eyes, for they were red and the skin around them was puffed. The lady had been weeping.

Helena Huntington was grave of mien, but this might have been caused by the occasion, which, God knew, was grave enough.

87

"You know my father?" she asked.

Alan, doubtless, had been gawking like an oaf. This was wrong. Not even for an instant could he afford to seem to lose his self-possession. His very life depended upon it, not to mention hers. If ever they decided that he was bluffing and they made a rush. . . .

So he swept the hat from off his head and he clapped it over his heart, making a deep bow.

For a moment, then, his face was hidden. When he straightened he had recovered control of himself, and was smiling in a superior way.

"I do indeed, Mistress Huntington, and a fine upright gentleman he is too."

"He's well?"

"He was when I last saw him, only a few days ago, at Government House in Spanish Town. He told me then that you were returning soon, but he hoped that you would wait until after the war, for that he feared for pirates. He'd have the skins flayed off of these rascals here, of course, if he thought that they'd laid a hand on his daughter. Have they in any way, uh, soiled you, Mistress Huntington?"

She glanced right and left, and her mouth was dry. She might have the appearance of a Greek goddess, but she was every inch a woman of the world. She knew what he meant. She knew what her chances were of remaining unspoiled in this camp, where slavering men undressed her with their eyes.

"Not yet," she said dryly. "But it's as well, sir, that my father's emissary came so promptly."

He wasn't her father's emissary, but there seemed no need to argue this. He bowed again. He clapped his hat back on.

"They're beasts," he conceded, "but exceedingly stupid

88

beasts. They deserve only to be kicked in the face, and· it pains me to have to help them by taking you away."

"Help them?"

Thomas Meachum broke in. "What in hell are you talking about?" he demanded, though he must have known.

"You didn't stop to think," an unruffled Alan went on. "You forgot article seven of our brotherhood-of-the-coast agreement, now didn't you?"

They might have forgotten that article just at first, in the excitement of sacking *Wallingford,* but they had remembered it since, and with dismay, as he saw from their faces.

Meachum's men, like all the other pirates attached a tremendous importance to those articles by which they were supposed to be governed. Every other form of authority they had foresworn, for they were outcasts *par excellence,* men who had turned their backs to decency, to civilization; but their beloved written articles, perhaps for this very reason, loomed enormous in their thoughts. They would debate for hours the meaning of a given clause or phrase in them. The articles, which each had solemnly vowed to obey, were their government, their king, their Bible and code.

Article seven, in this instance, had its counterpart in every such piratical compact. It was to be found in one form or another in all of them; and in many it was the first. It provided, simply, and succinctly, that no woman of any sort might for any reason or on any pretext whatsoever be even for a little while attached to the band in any capacity. It wasn't a moral scruple that had brought this about, nor was it the superstition common to all sailors that women aboard ship are unlucky. It was the lesson of experience, the story of the past. If any pirate was permitted to bring along his doxie, even for only a few days, there would soon be knives drawn, and the band, doubtless with a great deal of bloodshed, would be broken up.

"You ain't bound by those articles any more!" cried Meachum.

"No, but you are!" Alan countered. He looked around. "All of you!"

After that he ignored them, or appeared to. He motioned toward the Moses.

"So if your ladyship will accompany me, I'll have you back at the plantation within a couple of days, the winds willing."

Here she might have spoiled everything, dooming both of them to mutilation, shame, and death. Had she hesitated for an instant, everything would have been lost.

But she rose to the occasion. She was magnificent, a queen.

Graciously she gave Alan her hand.

"Thank you," she said.

That hand was trembling, but only Alan knew it. Helena never stumbled as she stepped into the boat, and when she sat, seemingly serene, in the sternsheets, it was upright. She did not deign to turn her head, but like Alan seemed to pay no heed to the others.

Alan was careful not to catch a crab, yet neither did he dawdle. There must be, now, neither undignified, revealing haste nor yet the frittering away of a single precious second.

It was hard to row at an ordinary pace, but he did it. It was hard not to look up, to see whether any gun was leveled at him, but he kept his gaze on the space between his feet.

As soon as he dared, when he figured that the Moses was far enough from shore so that his lips would not be visible, he started to talk to her in a low, encouraging voice.

"It was a damned nice thing for a while there, Mistress

Huntington. But I think we've brought it off. You were wonderful. If only your father could have—"

She slipped off the seat. She toppled forward, falling to the bottom of the boat. She had fainted.

9

THE *maître d'armes* would not hear of masks. He had them hung on his walls, as part of his professionalism, but he refused to use one or permit Alan to wear one.

"No, no! The days when a man might lose an eye or a few teeth at a lesson, they are past. Excepting among the Italians, with their long old-fashioned rapiers, and with their grunts and snorts, and their stampings and flourishes. Well, if you wish to dance about like an Italian, *poof!* Then this is not the place for you."

He tiptoed across the strip like a ballet dancer: you could almost hear the swish of the tutu, and it was hard to remember that this mincing midget had killed four men in affairs of honor.

"The French," he threw over a shoulder, "fence like gentlemen."

He was small, though wondrously supple, and he was exacting about the politenesses of the sport, which he preferred to call "the preparation." There were times, Alan mused, when he was more like a dancingmaster than a fencingmaster.

In the beginning he had put Alan through a series of shadow lunges and parries, counting aloud, and waggling his hands from the wrists for all the world like a teacher leading a class of children in song: "*Tierce, carte! Tierce, carte! Tierce, carte!* And now, prime position! Ah!" Alan, however, had grown past this, and since his return to town as a hero he was engaging in real bouts with this redoubtable, peppery, precise, small man.

"You are long. Your reach is more than mine. So do not feint so many times. Threaten more. Threaten the eyes."

MAROONED

"With you wearing no mask?"

Exasperated, the *maître* stamped his foot.

"I can defend myself! I tell you threaten, monsieur, threaten!"

Both stepped back when they heard a clatter of wheels on paving stones—the *salle* was located directly on the plaza—and by glancing through the windows they saw the upper part of the government coach.

That would be Colonel Swartout. Perhaps the lieutenant-governor was a poor horseman, or, more likely, he took the coach to be a symbol of power. It happened too that Thomas Handasyde, the real governor—if his reappointment was ever confirmed—disliked that cumberson vehicle, which he thought ostentatious and only to be used for purposes of high state. Thus Colonel Swartout was permitted his show.

Alan glanced at M. Boulanger. The *maître d'armes* in fact was much more than that. He was a social arbiter in Jamaica, a thermometer to read the temperature of the *haute monde*, the elite, a weathercock to tell which way the winds of fashion blew. He was punctilious, conscientious, and usually right. When he took his walk of a morning you could deduce the exact social importance of each person he passed by the depth to which he bowed or the height to which he lifted the tricorne from his head. You could even tell this by the comparative warmth or coolness with which he greeted his pupils, most of whom he bullied unmercifully.

Just now, Alan noted, M. Boulanger was by no means eager to be visited by the lieutenant-governor, an honor that would have delighted him a little while ago. This meant something. Did it mean that Colonel Swartout was going down, or that Alan Waite was coming up? Or did it mean both?

MAROONED

Almost with a sigh M. Boulanger put away his blade.

The door was opened, and Colombo ceremoniously announced his master, who strode in.

The lieutenant-governor, himself no fool, noticed the coolness of the proprietor, and he gathered from it that M. Boulanger resented this interruption. Swartout was touchy about such things. He knew that he was not well liked; popularity was not a thing he ever had hoped for, or courted. Nevertheless it irked him to see Alan Waite abruptly become —as a result of one lucky feat—a public hero, acclaimed all over the island, cheered whenever he showed his face. In his official capacity, as acting governor, Colonel Swartout had extended formal thanks and commendation to Alan for that feat. But his private thoughts were something quite different.

This young whippersnapper no longer worked and lived at the Flying Fish in Port Royal, though Swartout still suspected him of visits to that place, and to Nora. These days, since his sensational return, Alan Waite was living in the town residence of Henry Huntington, a palatial establishment as establishments in Kingston went. He was very brave in his new clothes, bought, no doubt, with part of the reward money a grateful father had bestowed upon him. In Swartout's eyes anyway, he strutted—though admittedly he always had been a cocky lad. Worse, he was at the moment monopolozing Mistress Huntington.

The white women of Jamaica were neither numerous nor of a notable beauty. The air did something to them, or perhaps, it was the sun. Anyway, whatever they might once have been, after a few months in the colony they came to be wan, all of them, and touched by a curious pallor. They sagged. They even peeled.

MAROONED

You might feel sorry for those ladies, but you'd hardly be drawn to them. With Helena Huntington it was different, was indeed quite the reverse. If she ever had had that unbecoming Jamaican complexion, the years in England, in a more vigorous, more violent climate, had driven it away, substituting or perhaps restoring a youthful ruddiness. She gleamed. She glowed.

This alone—aside from her charm, her availability in a place where unattached women were almost unknown, and the opulence of that father whose only child she was—would have been enough to endear her in Colonel Swartout's mind. Miss Lofts was all right for a certain purpose—indeed she was damned good that way—but the colonel felt himself drawn to the sprightly, lovely newcomer. But when would he ever come upon her alone? Always that peacock, young Waite, was by her side or at least within whistle. Colonel Swartout did not like it.

All of this was patent in his face, in his expression, as he stepped into the *salle d'escrime* and stopped short, seeing Alan. He didn't try to hide it.

Alan bowed.

The colonel did not respond.

"Oh? I see you've already got a pupil."

"I am always at your service, excellency."

"Well, I just happened to be passing and thought I might step in for a little exercise. But if—"

The *maître* had an inspiration.

"Why don't you two engage in a bout? It might be amusing."

"Eh?"

Swartout seemed startled. Until this time, though he had seen and commented sarcastically upon Alan's sword, he

95

never had thought of Alan, genuinely, as a gentleman. But evidently Boulanger considered him to be such. The thought of crossing steel with Alan, literally, had never occurred to the acting governor. Now, like the *maître*, he began to think that it might be amusing. After a moment he nodded.

"All right," he said.

He took off his periwig and coat. He worked off his shoes and tugged on pantofles of the same sort that Alan was wearing. He seized a gauntlet.

Alan would have preferred to specify masks, but he did not dare.

These three now had the *salle* to themselves, Colombo having returned to his box. The street sounds were muted here. For once it was not raining, and the light was good.

Alan Waite saluted formally, properly, as he had been taught to do. Swarthout had no patience with such fanciness, and without any pause he attacked.

M. Boulanger had said that the French fence like gentlemen. But Swarthout was not French. Nora called him the best blade in the English Army. Nora might not have been qualified to judge, but undeniably the man was brilliant, and he was very fast. His attack seemed overenthusiastic, even wild, but there was calculation behind it, as Alan learned. His point always was in line. He never left himself open. And when he went in he went in all the way, without any preliminary, telltale feint or half-lunge

The foils of course were buttoned, but they were made of stiff steel, and when at the end of two bouts Alan announced apologetically that he feared he did not have time for more sword play this afternoon his right ribs and right arm were throbbing and pulsing from the hits. He himself had got in two ripostes, rather to his own surprise. All the other touches had been Swartout's. "Touch" was a technical term: in fact those touches had been severe, vindictive pokes, and they hurt—and would hurt.

Alan bowed.

The colonel nodded negligently, then turned to M. Boulanger.

"Damn it, man, I'm only beginning to warm up. Could ye give me some opposition, eh?"

When a few minutes later, sore, sweaty, feeling foolish, Alan Waite let himself out of the academy, steel was again slithering against steel, musically, behind him. He should have lingered to watch these two experts, to study their styles, but he didn't.

Almost as though at a signal, as though it had been waiting for him to step into the plaza, the sun came out.

And then he spied Helena Huntington coming toward him. She did not run, but she did quicken her step and waved.

Alan forgot the sore spots.

When he returned from the island rescue it was as though he had stepped into another world. It was as though he was on a stage, blinking in the glare of the footlights, stared at and studied by many half-seen persons, his every movement watched, his syllables critically repeated. He was a public figure now. He was a legend within his own lifetime.

If this had its advantages, it had disadvantages too.

It was heady, exhilarating. It warmed his heart. It was good for his vanity to be pointed at and praised, to have strangers arrest him in the street and ask for his advice. If he had been cocky before, as Colonel Swartout believed, it was a posture of defense. It had expressed an inner uncertainty. But now he could swagger, and he did.

MAROONED

There were more material benefits. With his newly won prestige he could and successfully did insist upon more guns for *Lively Lass;* and in spite of a shortage of seamen, he was able to command a larger and notably more capable crew. He ate better and drank better at the Huntingtons than ever before in his life. He had credit in any shop in Spanish Town, Port Royal, or Kingston. Not that he needed such credit, for his purse, thanks to Henry Huntington's generosity, was well lined; but it was good for his soul to know that he could have it any time he asked.

The disadvantages were equally patent, and they were irksome. A public idol *is* public. During the first fine fervor of adoration and acclaim his life cannot be called his own. Privacy is his no longer, until the people tire of him. He *is* on a stage, and he must strut and posture as convention dictates, lest he be hissed.

This demand for conformity applied with extra emphasis to his relations with Helena Huntington. For she shared his glory, if glory it could be called. With him she had become a colonial sweetheart, and as such she had scant time to herself. She was up on that stage with Alan. Her beauty, her reappearance after four years, the romantic, dramatic circumstances of her rescue from the ruffians of the Meachum gang—these appealed to a public that ordinarily had little to talk about. She often appeared in the streets and in the shops with her savior, handsome, strapping young Captain Waite, the pirate-chaser. They were cheered and congratulated to a point of fulsomeness.

Nor did this attitude, annoying to both of them, appear to wane. Today, for example, though they had been back for almost a week, it was as blatant and troublesome as ever. They were both looking forward to the morrow, when, Helena having filled out her new wardrobe, they would, with Henry Huntington, start for the Huntington plantation, there to spend a few weeks of quiet.

Alan had retrieved the girl but not her clothing. Restored to her father's arms, Helena had nothing but the gown she stood in. This must be righted immediately; and it was no small reason for the public's delight in her that Helena had spent the week in a flurry of shopping, piling up great masses of brocade, lace, silks, muslin, always with Captain Waite at her side.

But it was finished now. This shop was the last, that length of cloth the final purchase. He would make final arrangements for the maintenance of *Lively Lass*, which rode at anchor just off Port Royal on the other side of the bay. Tomorrow they would start for the country.

At home or here, Alan never had been far from the waterfront. He had never seen a sugar plantation or any other kind of plantation, except from afar. Yet even keener than his expectation of getting to know the Huntington grinding-mills was his expectation of getting to know the Huntington heiress. He said as much, in effect, when he left her at her doorstep.

Passersby even here paused to admire the pair, and Alan obediently gave one of his deepest, most expert bows, sweeping his tricorne low, dropping his eyes in reverence. But there was no banter in his voice.

"Soon the curtain will come down, ma'am, and I think that neither of us will weep on account of that."

"Aye."

She tossed him something that might almost have been a grin, wrinkling her nose. But immediately afterward she was conventionally the flirt again, and tapped him with her parasol.

"La, sir, don't you be late for dinner!"

Carefully placing his tall silver-topped cane, and acknowledging salutations right and left, he strolled back to the bay. He reflected that he could even have, if he wished, that showy appendage of a town gentleman, a hulking attendant, a bodyguard. Lemuel Gray, the hand who had once thought of mutiny, was Alan's slave now. Anybody who could whip *him*, Lem reasoned, must be something like a god, and should be worshipped. Despite his fear of the press gangs that roamed the island, Lem would have followed Alan ashore and all around town if Alan had permitted this. But Lem was overzealous, always fearful lest somebody hurt Alan, and too quick with those enormous red fists. He embarrassed Alan, who, however, did put him in charge of the Moses boat with the title of coxwain.

Alan took a skimmer across the bay, and walked along the Port Royal waterfront past the shipyards to a point opposite the anchored *Lively Lass*. Lem had seen him, and was prompt to put out with the Moses. Just as the nose of that craft nudged the quay a small, wizened, oldish man seized Alan's wrist.

"Look, cap'n, could you give me a berth, eh? I'll work hard."

Without looking at him, Alan, who was getting used to being accosted by strangers, nodded to the shipping in the bay. There must have been close to fifty vessels, of all kinds and sizes, waiting for one of the warships to scrape together enough men to make up a crew and go along as escort to the convoy which was getting ready to leave.

"Any mariner that isn't lazy could get a berth," Alan said. "They're all short-handed, every one of 'em."

"Aye, and have the damned pressers nap me, afore I got to the first one?"

"Why apply to me, then?"

"Well, I haven't even got a knife to fight them pressers off with, and damn it, man, *you* ought to know that."

Gasping, Alan spun upon him.

"*Lennie Harris!*"

By this time Lem Gray had scrambled out of the tender and he 'seized Harris by the back of the neck so hard that the little man squealed.

"Take your hand off the captain, ye stinky rat!"

Alan interposed.

"That's all right, Lem. Let him go."

"I'll throw him in the drink!"

"No. Let him go. He's an old shipmate of mine."

And to Lennie: "What the devil are you doing ashore here?"

The pirate shook himself, glaring sideways at Lem. "Ducking press gangs mostly. And trying to find you. Can we get out of here? What about going aboard?"

"Of course."

10

THE LIEUTENANT-GOVERNOR brushed it aside with a quick impatient gesture, as though it were a cobweb he had walked into in the dark.

"Rubbish! Even if he has joined up with a French privateer, as you say this deserter of yours told you, why should he descend upon Port Royal of all places?"

"There's a might of loot in that warehouse," Alan reminded him.

Another impatient hand wave.

"But Port Royal's their own stamping-ground! Where else've they got to go? They wouldn't sack their own hideaway!"

"It *was* their stamping-ground," Alan corrected. "It *was* their hideaway. It isn't any more. These new regulations aren't very popular, you know, colonel."

"They weren't meant to be."

"Of course. But the pirates rebel. Merchants squawk when something seems to step on their mercantile toes, don't they?"

Swartout almost grinned. "They do."

"Then why shouldn't pirates? Or rather, people near to pirates?"

"Are you trying to justify piracy, Waite?"

"No, I'm only trying to explain it."

"I see. And that's useful, I guess. But there'll be no change. I have my orders from London. I am to make it hard for pirates to operate in these parts. And I will."

Standing there, looking down at him, Alan Waite wondered yet again about the lieutenant-governor. Everybody else in Jamaica was doing the same. How sincere was Swartout in his fulminations against theft on the high seas? Nora Lofts had averred that he sought rather to perpetuate piracy, at least as long as he had an indirect financial stake in it. According to her, he was profiting from the activities of such men as Tom Meachum—profiting more than the pirates themselves, and at no risk. This could be true. Much that Alan had seen and heard seemed to confirm it.

Colonel Swartout was in his dress uniform this evening, and he wore all his medals. Evidently he was about to go to some state function. Yet bright as he was, he could scarcely have outshone the room in which he sat, the magnificence of which had caused Alan to gasp. Nor was this Government House, the official residence at Spanish Town. It was a smaller house in Kingston that the lieutenant-governor had rented for his own convenience. Alan looked around again. Yes, this man was doing very well indeed.

Swartout glared at Alan now, his eyes as dark and hard as they had been not many hours ago in the fencing academy. It was disconcerting to be stared at that way. It was almost like being stabbed.

"Would he be that bold anyway, this horrendous Thomas Meachum?"

"Not alone, no. But if he found somebody to pitch in with him he would. And my friend tells me that this has happened. An accidental meeting, but a happy one. Off Petit Guaves."

"And so Meachum and this Frencher—what was his name? Senac?—they swore to a compact?"

"Not yet. But they will. That's been Meachum's pet idea for a long while, and he's almighty persuasive about it—to join up with a French privateer and sack Port Royal."

"He may have had other ideas since you last saw him. I mean, admitting that you ever did see him?"

"Oh, I've seen him all right! But Tom Meachum wouldn't

have two thoughts at one time. He lacks the intelligence."

"Umph!"

"I quite agree, sir. But remember, he'd get a heap of help here, if he was to send in a few men like this Lennie Harris—not that that's why Lennie is with us! There's a great deal of sympathy for piracy, over there on the other side of the bay, sir."

"You seem to know pretty much about how those people feel, over there."

"Why shouldn't I? I live among 'em."

"You mean you used to live among 'em. From all I hear, you're really living on Mr. Huntington, here in town, right now."

Alan Waite had no wish to talk about the Huntingtons with this man, and he turned away.

"I hear that you're even going out to spend some time at his plantation?" the colonel pursued.

"Yes. We leave tomorrow."

Alan strolled over to the windows, which were open. This was on the upper floor, and the windows were very large, for the better catching of air, as the ceiling was high.

It seemed in the first hush of this tropical night as though all the world out there consisted of vessels. The bay, near at hand, was crowded with them, hardly visible now. The air was filled with their furtive but unmistakable sounds—squeals and squeaks, the ringing of faraway bells, calls, commands, curses.

"Besides, we've got guns out there to protect us," the colonel said.

"Yes. All of them mounted in toward Kingston, to cover the channel. What about an attack from the sea side?"

"Impossible!"

MAROONED

"I'm damned if I see why."

"And I'm damned if I see why I put up with you, Waite. But still, you're part of our protection too, whenever you don't happen to be traipsing across country in pursuit of a rich man's daughter. And for that matter," the colonel added, with massive sarcasm, "we have the Navy."

Alan sniffed.

"Sure. Three old fourth-rates. Only one of them fit to take the seas. The other two have practically no guns left and no men to man 'em anyway. Wringley's seen to that."

Henry Wringley was captain of *Sapphira*, the least disgusting of the warships at Kingston. He would escort the scores of merchantmen up through the Florida Strait and across the northern Atlantic to Home. He would be a rich man if he made it. But Colonel Swartout here would be rich anyway. Swartout took his money in advance.

Alan turned away with a sigh, a shrug.

"Well, if I can't convince you—"

"I didn't say that. All I said was that I'd take it up later. I'll consider it. But there's no need for that as long as Wringley is here. Of course, maybe he'll never get enough men to sail?"

"He's sure trying hard enough."

At the door Alan bowed, as was customary. The colonel waved him away.

In the entrance hall downstairs, a large one, Colombo stood beside the street doors, holding a candle. Halfway to him, Alan had a corner of his eye caught by a figure crossing a corridor that led laterally from this foyer. He turned. He squinted.

It was Nora Lofts.

She wore very little, and she had the movement of a hovering bird. Probably she had been making for the necessary room when she saw Alan.

Nora seldom was startled, and still less often did she let it show. She seemed glad to see Alan. She took a step forward, still unseen by Colombo. She almost smiled.

He went to her.

"Another cup of chocolate, I suppose?"

"Why, of course. It's more convenient here. But when it got dark the colonel thought I'd better stay the night. You never know what you're going to run into, out there in the street."

"Yes. The press gangs might even nap you, they're so desperate."

She put a hand on his arm.

"Alan, you haven't been out to see me, since you came back."

"I thought I—"

"It's all right. I know. Great God, you're seen with her often enough."

He made no reply.

"And maybe it's just as well, Alan. We were getting too, well, fervent. It was always a little too good to be true, now wasn't it?"

That caught at his throat, and his eyes were misted. Fortunately there was nobody but her to see those eyes, for Colombo and his candle were not now in sight.

"She's pretty, Alan."

"Is she?"

Nora laughed, deep in her throat.

"What a stupid thing to say!"

She edged closer to him, and the smell of her skin was strong.

"You mustn't worry about me. I'm used to it, Alan. After

all, I'm in the business. But well, give me one more kiss!"

His pulses throbbing, his hands scrabbling wildly, he seized her.

There was a step behind him. He released her and turned.

Colonel Swartout had come downstairs. He stood in the middle of the entrance hall, facing their way. He was leaning forward a little. He could certainly see that somebody was there, but whether he could make out Nora's face Alan did not know. She whispered something that was meant to re-assure, and she disappeared through a door by which no one would dare to follow her.

Alan was in a cul-de-sac.

He walked out to the entrance hall, crossed it to the street doors, and turned there to make another small bow.

"Good night again, sir," he said.

Colombo threw open the doors.

The colonel nodded his head, just barely. There was again in his eyes that murderous light. He *had* seen!

"Don't get hurt," he called.

The Huntington plantation house, twenty-some miles from Kingston, was not pretentious, not grand. Rather, it was square, solid, comfortable, a handsome building made of light-gray stone that was not in itself lovely but was laid out in classically severe lines. It was a curious mixture of styles, that house. No ivy clung to its walls, but it was shaded by wide-spreading, scarlet-blossomed *flamboyante* trees. The garden, murmurous with bees, was as prim as any old maid, and except for its large size might have been the garden of a country house in Kent or Essex. Yet it was surrounded by a hedge of hibiscus that, while well clipped, was a riot of color. The house itself was comparatively cool, and though it was packed with shadows it was by no means gloomy. There were two stories to it, and on three sides of each ran deep verandas.

Behind the house a windmill creaked, ducks swam in a pond of indeterminate dimensions, and smoke sauntered out of a·pipe that emerged from the peaked roof of a kitchen made of bamboo.

The outbuildings were numerous. It startled Alan to learn that such a plantation, commercially devoted to sugar, was in fact a little civilization by itself. There was a huge and ugly grinding-mill, with two tall black stacks that spouted smoke. And there were all manner of shops and mills and storehouses, not to mention kennels, stables, and a barn. The overseers' quarters and the slaves' quarters, extensive, showed signs of careful upkeep.

The kitchen-garden was a triumph, though with its homely French beans and its rows of smug cabbages exactly spaced it looked as out of place in these exotic surroundings as did the flower garden in front. People, Alan suspected, came from miles around just to look at that vegetable garden, verily a work of art.

The plantation itself, including all of its buildings and fields, was located on a flat plain, not remarkable, and in truth rather drab and dusty. But to the north, and close at hand, were the Blue Mountains, a range that to Alan appeared a dark, jungle green. These mountains were beautiful, and he gawped at them. But Henry Huntington shook a heavy head.

"The Maroons."

"They hide there?" Alan asked.

"Well, they might. They've been glimpsed a few times,

from a distance. But you never can be sure of a Maroon.
They're like shadows. Just about that substantial."

"I see."

The fear that gnawed at the heart of every manager of a
sugar plantation, Alan knew from hearsay, was a slave uprising. It was one reason, perhaps the principal one, that the
colonial militia was so preposterously weak and unreliable.
No matter what the pressure, no matter how big the fine to
be imposed, men simply would not come in from the country
for drill, much less for service, they were so afraid to leave
their estates unguarded. Therefore the militia—as Tom
Meachum well knew—consisted of a few senile ex-Army officers croaking commands to a handful of clerks and shop-
keepers.

To have, on top of this, the fear of a Maroon raid—and
when the Maroons struck they left nothing but ashes—must
have made Henry Huntington a mighty apprehensive man.
Alan wondered why he did not move back to England, leaving a paid agent in charge of this plantation, himself simply
raking in the profits, the way most of the so-called "planters"
did. Certainly Henry Huntington could afford it.

Unless they were inspired from the outside, as by the
Maroons, it seemed to Alan that the slaves of the Huntington
plantation were hardly likely to go on a killing rampage. They
looked a docile lot. They could not be expected to sing and
frolic; surely they would not *enjoy* what they were doing.
But neither did they show resentment. They greeted Henry
Huntington gravely, if not smilingly, some of them even touching the palmetto hats they wore. Huntington, always a man
of reserve, was not effusive with them, but he was thorough,
inquiring about their condition, examining their kitchens and

MAROONED

their sleeping quarters, visiting their hospital. He took infinite pains about all this, asking many questions.

Certain it was that if at any time the slaves of the Huntington plantation, for whatever reason, did decide to rise in revolt, if ever they were filled with the frenzy induced by mob action, so that they didn't care how many of them were killed, it would be an easy matter for them to take over the whole place, burn every building, kill the overseers and the master, rape many times and at last slaughter Helena, and escape into the hills, there to seek out the Maroons, whom they would join. The nearest plantation house was almost six miles away, and the white managers there, like those here, were outnumbered by slaves at least forty to one. Alan shuddered when he thought of it. No wonder Henry Huntington was so somber a man!

It was not so with Huntington's daughter. Alan had supposed that she would take several days, at least, to unpack and supervise the putting away of her newly purchased finery, and he didn't hope to see much of her except at mealtimes. But she was ready in a few hours, and starry-eyed. She went with them on the first, preliminary tour of inspection, asking many questions, greeting old acquaintances. The slaves treated her very much as they treated her father, though with a touch more of curiosity. And if there were no smiles, neither were they any scowls.

The second day, while Huntington busied himself with his overseers, Helena and her guest, mounted, went farther afield. However, they did not then go beyond the limits of the Huntington plantation, and they returned in plenty of time for dinner.

The day after that, Alan's third at the plantation, these two rode up into the Blue Mountains.

MAROONED

It was done at her insistence, though Alan was willing enough and even eager, his only fear being that he might tumble, for he was a poor horseman. It was Henry Huntington who objected, and who only consented at last when Alan promised to take with him a fully loaded and primed pistol, along with his sword.

These conditions hardly jibed with a soporific atmosphere.

The sword was well enough, but Alan was not happy about the pistol. They were tricky things at best, those pistols, and likely to explode at a jog. Alan, in the hills, would have all he could do to stay in saddle, without having to watch a touchy piece of mechanism that might at a moment's misuse shoot the toes off his foot, frightening his horse into a panic. But he consented. He wanted to much to be alone with Helena.

The previous day they had chattered pauselessly, getting to know one another. This morning they were quiet. Once they had left the plain and started to climb, indeed, they needed all their wind. Even Helena, an accomplished horsewoman, found the going hard.

Alan was amazed at the coolness of the forest. Entering it was more like going down into a cellar than going up a mountain. The shadows were thick, as were the moss and creepers. The footing was treacherous. When at last they came to an outjutting of rock covered with moss and soft grass, a spot with a breathtaking view of the plantation, the plain, and the exquisitely blue Carribean, they were tired. They threw themselves on the ground. They ate the bread and cheese that they had brought, and drank from a flask of wine.

The scene was misted in a tropical haze, and utterly silent. It did not look real. It was like an enchanted land entoiled in some spell. The only thing that moved down there was a

111

tiny horseman, galloping toward the base of the mountains. Why gallop on a day like this, in a place like this? It was mighty silly of him, whoever he was. The dust stood out behind him like a yellow-brown fan. He leaned low over the neck of his mount.

Suddenly Helena asked, "What are you thinking of?"

"You," he answered promptly and honestly.

There was some silence.

"And you?" he asked.

"La, sir," she started, and paused. It was a weak attempt at gaiety, the first he had heard her use since they left Kingston. "If I told you what I think of you there'd be no containing this fool by my side."

Here was conventional flirtation, in itself meaningless, and she had retreated into it as into a refuge, proving that she was afraid.

Alan sat up, his heart thumping.

She still was staring down over the plain, where the foolish horseman no longer was visible. She did not swivel her eyes toward Alan as he started to lean around her, but she surely sensed that his mouth was coming.

He lay back again, after the kiss, as exhausted as though the intimacy had been ultimate. But he did have strength to take her hand. And she was trembling. Her shoulders were shaking! She was in tears!

He sat up with a jerk.

"Helena!"

"Alan!"

There was a step behind them, a rustle of leaves. Alan sprang to his feet, reaching for his sword. The horse pistol was in its saddle holster thirty feet away.

But this was not a Maroon. It was one of the attendants at

112

MAROONED

Government House, a mousy man whose face was familiar to Alan Waite. He handed Alan a message from the acting governor, Colonel Thomas Swartout. He had been instructed, the messenger explained, to deliver it personally to Master Waite, and at the plantation house they had directed him out here.

Alan faced Helena Huntington, whose face was turned away, doubtless to hide the tears. Alan made a leg. The messenger must be remembered.

"If you will forgive me, ma'am?"

She waved a negligent hand.

"La, sir, of course! Read on, read on!"

Wringley, the acting governor had written, was making a wild last-minute round-up, determined to get away with his convoy, and there was danger that through a legal technicality he might be able to impress the whole crew of *Lively Lass*. Would Captain Waite come instantly? It was too complicated to explain in a hasty note like this, but there was a chance that he might turn the trick.

"I must go back to Kingston."

"Immediately?"

"I'm afraid immediately."

11

He had no further chance to talk to her alone. On the way back to the plantation Swartout's messenger trailed them, and the actual good-by, late in the afternoon, was witnessed by her father and half a dozen house servants, besides that same messenger, who had accepted an invitation to stay overnight.

"You will come back, sir?" she asked giving him her hand.

"Of course I'll come back!"

They were worried about his late departure: it would be dark before he reached Kingston. He laughed at this. When a matter of hours might mean a crew he would not be talked into tarrying until dawn. Colonel Swartout, he believed, would never have written such a message unless the situation was serious. This move on the part of Captain Wringley, Alan knew, had been for some time in the cards. Folks at Kingston could see it coming. Even before the arrival of the lieutenant-governor there had been hard feeling between the Royal Navy on one side and the Army and the civilian government on the other. Swartout, at once an Army man and the acting head of the government, naturally was opposed to the Navy's power in these parts.

On the other hand, the colonel was making money out of the Navy by reason of the split escorting fees, and he must make at least a show of co-operating in the solution of the Navy's greatest local problem—a shortage of men. Whatever he did seemingly was not sufficient to satisfy Captain Wringley, a man who took himself and his service very seriously. The situation was even further complicated by the fact that Wringley was the highest able-handed Navy officer in this station (the admiral himself, the bucky, redoubtable Benbow, being in hospital at Port Royal with two broken legs and a high fever).

For some time, then, a storm had been brewing. It was freely predicted that Wringley would do just what he appeared now to have done—that is, at the last minute, just before sailing, having kept the day and perhaps even the hour of departure a secret, he would have his press gangs sweep up everything in sight. Before the hullaballoo died Wringley would be at sea. It was not likely that he would ever again be sent down to this Godforsaken stinking hole: his friends at Whitehall could see to that. And if what he did here in Jamaica, even in war time, was later declared to be illegal, why, what of that? Such a proceeding might hurt his pride, but it could hardly hurt his pocketbook. And it would take time—months, years—at such a great distance. Captain Wringley would be retired before it was settled.

Alan was not thinking of this, however, nor was he thinking of the fate of his men, as he should have been, when he departed from the Huntington house. He was thinking of Helena and of that kiss.

It had meant a lot to her, he was sure. She was not a giggling sort of girl. She would not flirt, except in public as a concession to the mode. Yet she had not put up any resistance. How much further would he dare to go, when he came back?

Henry Huntington had insisted again that Alan carry that huge pistol in his saddle holster. The road was not safe, Huntington said.

Alan scoffed at this.

"Why, the press gangs will have cleaned up every unfastened waif and stray long ago, but particularly tonight," Alan cried.

"It's the press gangs that I'm thinking of."

Alan guffawed. After all, he was a hero.

"You mean—" he jabbed his own chest with his own fore-finger—"you think they might try to press me?"

"You'd better carry that gun anyway," Henry Huntington said.

Alan had agreed, rather than lose time in argument, but he uncocked the cumbersome thing as soon as he got out of sight of the house, though he did leave the charge in it.

And in truth, just at first when the marines spread themselves before him and demanded that he dismount, he forgot all about the pistol.

This was just outside of Kingston, a town that showed few lights, though the evening still was young.

The marines had appeared, seemingly, from nowhere. There were four of them, their leader being a sergeant armed with a hanger, or short saberlike sword, that hung from his shoulder by a baldric. The others carried cudgels.

"We're looking for a man named Waite, who's a deserter from His Majesty's Navy," the sergeant said.

"My name is Waite," Alan replied, "but I was never in the Navy."

"This might be a good time for you to start," the sergeant said.

It was dark, and Alan couldn't see them well. By the same token, to be sure, they could not see him clearly. Yet he was amazed at their effrontry in halting a man on a horse.

A horse in Jamaica was proof of gentility. For all practical purposes there were only two kinds of horses on this island: worn farm animals shipped down from the Atlantic coast colonies such as Rhode Island and Connecticut, to be slaughtered for slave food; and mounts for gentlemen and ladies, riding horses. There were no plow horses, and not even in Kingston or in Port Royal were there dray horses, slave labor being as cheap as it was. The steed Alan Waite bestrode was one of the best in the Huntington stable, which meant that it was one of the best in this part of the world. Even a Royal Marine should see this.

Besides, Alan had a sword at his side.

"Get down," said the sergeant.

Alan frowned.

"Now see here," he began, "I happen to be on an important mission for Colonel Swartout. He's the acting governor of this colony, in case you hadn't heard."

"I've heard."

"If I am delayed for any reason at all . . . Well, if you can't believe me, I've got a letter here, written in his excellency's own hand, summoning me to his house in Kingston. I don't think that I should be delayed."

He touched his left waistcoat pocket, taking care to rattle the sword with an elbow as he did so.

"Would you care to read it?"

The sergeant shook his head. He was not interested in letters. Perhaps he couldn't read but didn't want the others to learn this? Or had he his orders?

"Get down," he said again.

It was then that Alan remembered the pistol. He was about to draw his sword, but he had doubts about its effectiveness in these circumstances. Alan had become a fair blade on the fencing strip at the academy, but he knew nothing about cavalry tactics, and it was not probable that this steed did either. "Don't show your teeth unless you can bite," goes an old Scottish saying. Alan Waite was a poor horseman at best, and these four marines didn't look like men who would be frightened away by the sight of a strip of steel. The pistol, though, might do the trick. He fetched it forth.

"Get out of my way," he said coldly, and cocked the thing.

The result was astonishing. The marines, at no spoken command, seemed to disappear as though fog had swallowed them, as though they had evaporated into thin air. For an instant Alan Waite really thought that he had pushed them into a panic.

Then his horse's rump was swatted hard and the horse, whinnying wildly, rose on its hind legs. Alan with his left hand grabbed the pommel of the saddle. The pistol in his right hand went off.

The explosion was terrific. It seemed to shake the whole world.

The horse bolted, but it didn't take Alan with it. Alan already was half-thrown when somebody from behind seized and unstirruped his right foot. He never had a chance to kick, much less to draw. He fell to the ground.

It knocked the wind out of him. He tried to roll away, for he guessed what was coming. But he was too weak. And these pressers knew their business. They were on him instantly.

Alan felt the blows—some of them. They didn't hurt much. It was a soft thudding, as though the cudgels were padded. It was almost apologetic. But the roar that filled his ears increased, and swelled. That black roar could not be denied. It was about to engulf him.

He tried to get his arms up, to protect his head.

That was the last thing he remembered.

When he recovered consciousness it was to find himself chained to an iron bar fastened to a mast. Here was a scene

of great activity, anthill-like, yet nobody paid any attention
to Alan Waite, who half-sat, half-lay on the deck, groaning, his
head a mass of bruises and dried blood. Seamen scurried past,
their pigtails abob. A lieutenant, brave in blue and froggery,
paced the quarterdeck as if he was counting the planks.
Gunners and gunners' mates fussed with their weapons. Hands
swabbed. Topmen brachiated. Midshipmen, mere midgets,
strutted, some with swords almost as big as themselves.

As for Alan, he might have been part of the deck itself, or
of the mast. It was as though these nautical ruffians were ac-
customed to the sight of a beaten man lying in chains, as
indeed they probably were. When Alan struggled to his
knees, and then to his feet, he tried, in a startlingly hoarse
voice, to accost some of these passers. It did no good. They
hurried on, looking scared. Evidently it was against regulations
to speak to a prisoner aboard His Majesty's brig-of-war *Sapphira*.

Alan wet his lips, shook his head and twisted around. It
was the first time he noticed the master-at-arms standing to
his back. He walked in front of Alan, his truncheon at his
side. He was long, lank and lugubrious, with warts on his
chin and tattoo burns on the backs of his hands. He belched.

"No, now, you can't look that way when I take you before
the captain," he fussed, shaking his head. "You're a mess."

"Well, get me some water, then."

Insisting that they'd got the wrong man, insisting too that
he had in his possession a letter from the acting governor, a
letter that would establish his innocence, Alan had demanded
to be taken before the captain himself, no less. To his own
great astonishment this wish was granted.

The master-at-arms was not an evil man, only unimagina-
tive. He caused water to be brought. Alan drank deep and

then, as best he could while in manacles, he washed. Not until then did the master-at-arms unlock the wrist and ankle irons. This showed an excess of caution, for though they were still in Kingston Harbor they were anchored a good half-mile from Port Royal, and Alan in his battered condition could never have dived overboard anyway.

The master-at-arms even helped to brush Alan off, and to straighten a sadly rumpled coat.

"It don't look right, for you to be like this in the presence of Captain Wringley. He's a proper gentleman, he is. Come along now."

The captain kept them waiting for more than two hours and the sun was low when at last they stepped between the marines posted before his cabin, two ramrods in scarlet. The sun flared through the ports and lighted the opposite bulkhead.

This was a very grand cabin, high-ceilinged for a ship, extending the whole beam of the brig. It gave forth a dark glow of mahogany.

The master-at-arms whipped off his hat. The two marines stepped into the cabin after them, and stood right behind Alan.

Sunlight fleered off a silver salver, a quill, the gently jiggling epaulettes on the captain's shoulders, most of all the intense light-blue of the captain's eyes, set in a face itself as red as a sunset. Those eyes were ice. The mouth was a steel-toothed trap. Captain Sir Henry Wringley was not, now, amused.

"Never mind reciting the charges, Pierce. They'd start with desertion, of course, and we won't accuse this man of desertion."

That, Alan supposed just at first, was because the captain

knew that he was lying and didn't wish a record made of such a lie.

"You are an old hand in the Royal Navy," the captain said, addressing Alan for the first time, "and you know what the usual punishment for desertion is: flogging through the fleet."

"Begging your pardon, sir," Alan started bitterly, "but I'm not an old hand in the Royal Navy. I've never served before, and I have no wish to serve now, and when Colonel Swartout hears about this—"

"Ah, yes. Pierce did say something about a letter. Well, I'll look at it."

He held out a languid hand.

Alan reached into his lower left waistcoat pocket. It was empty. So were all the other pockets. The kerchief remained, but that was all. The coins were gone, and so was the letter from the acting governor.

"Somebody's stolen it!"

"No doubt," the captain said dryly. Now his face turned hard and angry, and he waggled a finger at Alan. "You'd better consider yourself lucky that I'm going to press only a minor charge of being ashore without official permission. If you do your work properly after this, Waite, the rest will be forgiven. Of course, if you don't. . . ."

He shrugged and took up the pen. "Put him in irons."

Sometime during those seven days Alan figured one thing for certain: the whole thing was Swartout's doing. The acting governor had made a deal with Wringley. Those marines had been waiting for him. There was no other way to account for their presence outside of Kingston and their willingness to nap a man with a sword. They had known about that letter too, and had orders to get it. Thanks to Alan's own histrionics they had known just where to look.

That was why Alan had been admitted into the august presence of Captain Sir Henry Wringley. The captain, bluntly, was curious. He wanted a look at the man Tom Swartout had taken so much trouble to get rid of.

Oh, assuredly it was Swartout's doing! And Swartout, with his command of the machinery of government, together with the arrangement he undoubtedly had made with Wringley, would be able to forestall and perhaps even to frustrate a search. At least until the customary last-minute hitches had been surmounted and the convoy actually had sailed. After that nothing mattered, from Tom Swartout's point of view. It would take half a year at the very least for Alan Waite to get back to Jamaica, if he ever got back at all. Within half a year Colonel Swartout, having made his pile, would be ready to clear out.

Alan had been, frankly, surprised. He knew that Swartout was a vindictive man, and he rather believed with Nora Lofts that part of the reason for sending Alan out in command of *Lively Lass* was the hope that he would indeed backslide, reverting to piracy. When Alan didn't, when he returned to become a public hero, he could expect the colonel to take other steps. Alan might be set upon in some dark alley. He might be beaten, and even killed. But what Alan had not expected was to be impressed into the Royal Navy.

He had thought on this for seven days, now, and there was only one other thought in his mind: escape. In that week the *Sapphira* had stood still. Only this morning had they at last begun to move, and even now, it seemed to him, they were hove to, if not actually anchored, probably somewhere just outside of Kingston Harbor, perhaps waiting for the rest of the vessels to get into formation.

Now that they were out of the Harbor, Alan was released from irons, and allowed to work below. But at least he could glimpse something besides the black hold of the past week.

Alan had never dreamed that the land could look so lovely, that beaches could be such a dazzling white, the sea such a dazzling blue. *Sapphira* had taken an inside position—fairly close to the mouth of the Black River, someone told him. There were at least forty other vessels, all low in the water, anchored dangerously close together. In Alan Waite's opinion, which nobody had asked, it was a poor place for a rendez-vous. And nobody knew how long they'd stay, how long it would take for the Mosquito Coast fleet, for which they waited, to join them.

It was because he looked at it through a landsman's eyes, the eyes of one so recently bemused by a visit to a fine inland plantation, that Alan found the shore fair. In fact, those beaches were far away, to right and left. Directly ahead there was only a glum, dark, glowering swamp. He knew that it was the mouth of the Black River only because he'd been so told: there was nothing to mark the spot. Beyond, higher up, there were some fleecy coconut palms that fleered back the light of the sun, also a few dun-brown thatched huts that looked for all the world like haystacks, but he saw no column of smoke, no movement ashore.

The swamp was not much more than half a mile away, he calculated, and the only thing that moved between it and *Sapphira* was a patrol boat loaded with marines.

"It's a hell of a place," Alan grumbled. "Why didn't they stay in Kingston? Why didn't they wait for the Mosquitomen there?"

"That's what the merchants would've liked," said a seaman named Terret Ryan. "But it was too easy there to go over the side. They were deserting in droves, as fast as the press gangs could bring in new ones."

Alan chewed this.

"I thought most seamen couldn't swim," he said at last.

"Most of 'em can't, I reckon. But some can. And others'd hang onto a spar or a plank and take the chance of sharks, so long as they could find some sensible decent human beings if they did make it," went on Terret. "But there's nothing here except swamp and open hills—no place to hide."

Alan had selected the following Sunday for his escape.

He did not dare to wait any longer, for already they had been standing off the mouth of the Black River for two weeks.

It would be toward the end of the middle night watch, the graveyard watch, just before the early watch was turned out at eight bells, four o'clock.

The eye was least alert, least sure of itself, he reasoned, at dusk and at dawn, the periods of shifting light. But dusk, here in the tropics, was not as he had known it elsewhere: it was not a period of gradual fading, but an abrupt switch, when night swooped suddenly, in a rush, as though some celestial candle had been whuffed out. Dawn, on the other hand, streaky, sticky, slow.

The choice of a Sabbath also was well considered. The old skippers' cry of "No Sundays off soundings" did not apply to the *Sapphira*, for Captain Wringley was a very religious man. There was chapel, at which attendance was compulsory, for the one was esteemed as morally edifying as the compulsory attendance at flogging. And there were routine tasks. But a take-it-easy attitude prevailed.

MAROONED

His plan was perfectly simple, as it had to be, considering the means at his disposal.

The shore, the swamp part of it anyway, was little more than half a mile from *Sapphira*. There was no reef, and the intervening water, from the color of it, was deep. The breakers, in mild weather, were trifling. Sharks always followed ships, and Alan had to hope that once he was well away from the brig he would also be well away from the scavengers of the sea, which would stay close to the various vessels as they nuzzled for garbage. That space at night, also, would be patrolled. This too he had to chance. But there would be no moon: he had checked that. In the first wavering of dawn it would be hard for boatmen to detect one bobbing head.

For he meant to swim it. He could see no other way.

12

"THEN I'LL go in myself," said Helena.

Her father shook a sad head. He knew better than to try to dissuade her when she spoke in that voice, and he determined, weary as he was, to go with her. Kingston—as he knew so well, having just returned from there—was not a safe place since the convoy had gone.

The press gangs were hardly flavorsome, but at least while they operated they had kept the fear of God in the breasts of pimps, publicans, and cutpurses. Once they were gone, once the threat had been removed, deserters seemed fairly to crawl, like bugs, out of the woodwork. They were everywhere, celebrating their liberation, looking for trouble; they all needed money and weren't fussy about how they got it.

In the past it had been a custom to leave a small press gang after the sailing for the very purpose of napping these deserters when they sneaked out of hiding; but this time this had not been done, for Wringley needed every man he could get. The result was that Kingston, and even more so Port Royal, where Henry Huntington also had gone in search of Captain Waite, were not safe places for anybody, even in broad daylight.

"I wouldn't," he said weakly. "I can't imagine where you could look and ask where I haven't asked and looked."

There was at least one place where he hoped that she wouldn't go, not having heard of it. He himself, Henry Huntington, a conscientious man, had gone there; and at the Flying Fish in Port Royal he had asked, in vain, for news of Alan Waite. The one person who might know something of Waite's whereabouts, all were agreed, was the acting governor, Colonel Swartout. But Swartout refused to receive anybody, even Henry Huntington, who in consequence had returned to his plantation without so much as a rumor with which to comfort his daughter.

He assumed that she did not know about the Flying Fish. Well, *he* certainly wasn't going to tell her. Not that it would make any difference, once she had made up her mind.

"I'll go with you, then" he said.

"All right."

Already she was ordering her riding skirt to be laid out, her horse to be saddled and brought around. She was about to start upstairs when a considerable clamor from the direction of the garden sent them both, puzzled, to a window.

The slaves on this plantation were well treated. It was never necessary to beat them into work, but they would quit the cane fields whenever something attracted their attention. They had done so this afternoon, scores of them trailing a tramp, a wanderer, upon whom they gaped with undisguised curiosity—as well they might, for they had never before seen anything like him.

Neither had the Huntingtons seen anything like him, they realized, as they watched this scarecrow enter the garden, leaving the slaves at the gate. He was tall; he was gaunt, spare. He wore no wig, and his hair, unkempt, not long enough to be clubbed and sacked, was matted with leaves and twigs. His feet and his lower legs were bare and very dirty. His breeches were torn in many places, as was his shirt. He was a white man, evidently, but his face had been reddened by sun and wind, and bushy whiskers ran riot across his face.

Nevertheless, and though from the dust upon him he must have come a long way, his step was sprightly. When he saw the Huntingtons in the drawing room window he gave them a gay wave.

127

MAROONED

"It's Alan!"

"My dear, you must be—"

But she had gone. She sped out of the house, down the garden path, and unhesitatingly threw herself into the arms of the newcomer.

"Well, I'll be damned," whispered Henry Huntington.

For it *was* Alan Waite.

The man at the window was touched, and as much startled by his daughter's behavior as by the identity of the newcomer. He had known, to be sure, that Helena was very fond of Alan Waite, as well she might be. And he had known that she was worried about his disappearance. But he'd never supposed that she would cast herself upon him like this. He shook his head. He went out.

Alan himself was astonished and touched. He kissed her again, tenderly, disregarding the slaves clustered behind him. He smiled down at her.

"Just like a homing pigeon, eh?" he said.

Though he sagged, he was in excellent spirits, and he would have stayed just like this for a long time, had not Henry Huntington arrived upon the scene.

"My God, man, what have you been doing?"

"For the past five days, walking," Alan answered with a grin. "Well, mostly nights. In the daytime I'd hole up in some cane brake. I never thought it safe to approach a plantation house until I'd checked with you, sir."

"Now that was very sensible of you. But come inside. Lord, man, you need soap and water!"

"Now that's the truth. There's a lot to tell, but first could I maybe get inside of a hot bath and then outside of some cold punch? I'd sure appreciate it."

MAROONED

"Dinner will be ready for you when you come down. And so will we."

Half an hour later Alan surveyed himself in a pier glass, and he beamed. His face, weather-roughened above, white below where he had only just shaved, might have been a bit startling when seen for the first time. But at least it was clean again. His hair had been cut, and he wore a small, dapper, well-powdered wig. Henry Huntington's clothes fitted him surprisingly well. The feeling of lace and silk was one that he had not forgotten, and he thrilled to it once more. Also, he had a sword at his side. He drew it and made a few passes.

"Thomas Swartout," he said softly.

It was about Swartout that his host asked him, as soon as he had descended.

"Are you sure he did it?"

"I haven't the slightest doubt. That message was in his own handwriting, and he knew that it was the one thing that would bring me on the run. By catching me just outside of the town, and just after sunset, he could be reasonably sure that it would not be reported. And he had this agreement with Wringley. What's happened to my men, by the way?"

"They were all right when I saw 'em yesterday in Kingston, though they didn't know what to do. Seems Swartout has issued a warrant for your arrest as a deserter from the militia."

Alan laughed at the irony of that. *Lively Lass* and all her crew theoretically were a part of the ridiculous Jamaican militia, which gave the acting governor the right to order them about.

"They get me coming and going, don't they?" Alan said.

This was the middle of the afternoon, the usual time for dinner in those parts, and the host, with a graceful wave toward the dining room reminded them of this.

"We want to hear it all, Helena and I both. But first, you must be starved?"

"I could eat," Alan conceded.

"Roast hare and current jelly, baked pompano with a foremeat of shrimps, oysters, and mushrooms . . ."

"Sounds better than raw land crab."

As they started for the dining room he slipped a hand into Helena's. Both were trembling. It was all too good to be true.

They never did get to that table. Another man was approaching the Huntington plantation house, approaching much faster than had Alan. He was a horseman, and dust swirled behind him. He came from the direction of Kingston.

They met this messenger on the veranda. He was so hoarse that it was hard to understand him.

"Meachum! . . . Port Royal's afire! . . . For God's sake, give me some beer!"

"I'd better go right away," said Alan Waite.

They saw the smoke for a long time before they got there. It was thick and black against a cobalt sky, and it rolled, wavering, toward them.

"Wind's off the sea," said Alan. "They could ride right up to a point just outside the pass, and then land on the sea side of Port Royal."

"That isn't possible!"

"You don't know Tom Meachum."

Helena was not with them. She had wished to go, but this time her father was adamantine.

The way—it could scarcely be dignified with the name of road—was crowded, but it was crowded not as might have been expected, with planters who hurried to get to the place of peril in order to protect their land from pirates. Rather,

130

the very contrary was true, and the bulk of the masses moved away from Kingston Bay, so that Alan and his companion virtually had to fight their way, several times being almost submerged in what amounted to a mob.

There was more than a touch of panic about this movement. A few actually ran, from time to time looking back over their shoulders as though they feared that they were about to be seized by the Devil, while even the less excited ones moved rapidly. Many obviously were townsmen, and carried or wheeled in barrows their valuables. Others, however, were planters. Henry Huntington grabbed one of these.

"See here, Walker, where're you going? Shouldn't you be looking after your militia duties?"

"My militia duties, Mr. Huntington, are out on my own plantation, as far as I'm concerned. Suppose those buccaneers decide to strike inland? Don't you think my blacks'd use it as an excuse to burn down all my buildings?"

"There ain't any buccaneers any more," Huntington argued. "These are pirates. They wouldn't get more than a mile from the sea if you prodded them with a pike. They hit and then they run away."

"Well, I don't want 'em running *my* way. So, let me past, please."

Still Henry Huntington held him.

"Walker, you'll get into trouble when Swartout hears of this. Don't you know he's acting commander-in-chief of the whole colonial militia?"

"I know he's acting a heap of things. He's been acting governor and acting treasury-emptyer ever since he landed here. And right now he's acting chief coward." Walker waved around him. "You think *we're* running away? Oh, no, Mr.

131

Huntington. We're only following our legal leader, that's all. *He* was the first to scamper."

"Harry Swartout run away?"

This was Alan. Walker glanced coldly at him.

"I don't know where else he is, sir, if he hasn't run away. It's sure that nobody can find him, and he didn't leave any orders."

"I don't believe it," cried Alan. "Swartout's a rascal, aye, but he's no milksop!"

Walker shrugged himself loose from Huntingtons' hand. He tugged at his rein.

"Why don't you tell him that then. If you can find him? But I know where I'm going."

He rode off.

The nearer to Kingston they got the greater became the confusion, the pushier and more urgent the crowd. Not again did they stop to talk, but they did gather from scraps of overheard conversation that Walker was right: Colonel Swartout had disappeared at the crucial moment, leaving behind him a great gaping void of uncertainty. These people were not all poltroons. They would have stood their ground, or many of them would. Given a chance, they would have responded to leadership. But there was no leadership. They didn't know where they stood, and instinct tugged at them to flee. The militiamen by and large might have been willing to obey their officers, howsoever inexpert, or inexperienced. But whom should the officers obey?

They learned further, as they got into the town itself, that the previous governor, who might still prove to be the proper governor when those commissions came from Home—if they ever did—had taken it upon himself to try to rally the militia officers at Kingston. This man, a planter himself, was well-known and generally well-liked in the colony. He didn't know whether he had the authority to organize resistance to the pirates, but in the absence of Harry Swartout he was willing to act as though he had.

"That's where I belong," said Mr. Huntington. "I know Tom Handasyde well, and I could help him."

"All right," said Alan. "But where I belong, naturally, is with my men."

Huntington regarded him gravely.

"Be careful now. Remember you're actually a fugitive from justice, in a manner of speaking. There's a warrant out for your arrest. You're wanted."

"I'm wanted where Tom Meachum is—to kill him."

"You haven't got a scrap of authority, remember that."

Alan grinned.

"Oh, yes I have." He tapped his sword. "It's right here."

The older man put a hand on Alan's forearm.

"Well, if you won't be careful for me or for yourself, then try to be careful for *her*, eh?"

Alan felt his face go hot, and he turned away.

"I'll be careful," he muttered.

The whereabouts of the lieutenant-governor might be unknown, but it was not so with the whereabouts of *Lively Lass*. Mr. Huntington, who had visited the vessel only the previous day to interview members of her crew, was able to tell Alan exactly where *Lively Lass* was anchored. It was easy to hire a gig.

The waterfront, indeed all of the Kingston side of the bay, was cluttered with small craft, so that it looked almost as crammed as it had looked before the departure of the convoy. Many of these craft were bumboats or gigs or cocks, but it was on this side too that there clustered all the skimmers, the fast, light-draft sloops that plied between Port Royal and Kingston with passengers or packages.

The channel itself was empty, save for the two decrepit warships, vessels that were falling apart for lack of mariners to man them even in port. Neither of these fourth-raters was making the slightest attempt to bombard the town of Port Royal, perhaps for fear of hurting friends, more likely because Wringley had stripped them of guns and gunners alike.

A few of the rusty old pieces still left in the Apostles' Battery on the hill behind Port Henderson, just across the entrance to the bay from Port Royal, occasionally gave forth a gutteral cough, a cloud of smoke. These could not have reached Port Royal even if that had been desired, and it was not likely that they could reach any of the piratical vessels lying just outside. The most the Apostles' guns could hope to do was set up a sort of sporadic barrage in the channel itself, thus discouraging the pirates from any attempt to force their way in—something that the pirates, if Alan Waite knew them, wouldn't have dreamed of doing anyway.

The only other gunfire came from the burning town itself, and this was the occasional crack of muskets, audible here, clear across the bay, by reason of that strong sea breeze. Audible, yes, but very faint: it sounded like the spickle of eggs frying on a stove. The smoke was unceasing, rolling up and north, blotting out the sun even over here.

The men of *Lively Lass* were overjoyed to see their skipper. They told him so. They slapped his back and pumped his hand. They babbled questions at him.

All the same, some of them looked dismayed when Alan ordered the anchor up and a course made for Sadoes, a hamlet on the same low sandy peninsula of which Port Royal formed the tip.

"We'll go in by the back door."

"But sir, we can't get there," cried Lemuel Gray. "It's too shoal."

"All right. Jettison those guns then."

The men stood appalled. These were good guns, nine of them now, four on each side and a bow-chaser, and Alan Waite had gone to extraordinary efforts to get them, using all of Mr. Huntington's influence and all of his own prestige as a hero. The wonder was that Wringley had not confiscated them in Alan's absence. To toss such weapons into the harbor seemed all but sacriligious.

"Well, go ahead. Roll 'em over! They can easily be salvaged later."

"But captain . . . sir—"

"God damn it, jettison those guns!"

A few minutes later, much lighter, scarcely more than a skimmer in themselves, they were making across the bay. If anybody watched them through a glass—which was improbable—he would have seen nothing to alarm him. No guns were run out. There were only a few men in sight. Alan had ordered the others to the forecastle. *Lively Lass* herself, though she would pass near to Port Royal, was making a rather crazy course for a point much farther down the spit, where for reasons of her own she would probably go aground. No cause for alarm there. No threat of attack. Just some madman.

The heat was terrific, and now they could hear sounds of the fire itself—the crackling of timbers, the crash of falling beams, the *whoosh* of roofs going up like so much dried hay.

The smoke was lower and thicker, and there were sparks in it now.

"Lennie, break out the pikes and cutlasses. One apiece, all around."

"You're going to *board*, skipper?"

"Of course we are. We can't expect 'em to swim out to us, now can we?"

"Me too? They'd tear me to pieces."

"No, you can stay here, keep her from drifting out. But all the others go."

"Aye, aye, sir."

Despite the fact that they could not even see the sky for the smoke, the water glowed with a color of its own, seemingly thrown up from below. This color was red—the reflection of flames, though some of it, too, might have been blood.

The bang of muskets was louder now, though there was not much of it. Muskets were tricky, dirty, unreliable instruments. Tom Meachum's men preferred to use cold steel when they went in. And the opposition over there in Port Royal must be trifling—no militia at all, probably, and only a handful of marines to guard the warehouse.

A body floated by. It was that of a middle-aged seaman, his eyes agoggle like the eyes of a frog, his throat cut from ear to ear. The eyes told the tale. The poor wretch had been tortured by means of powerful compresses across the forehead and temples, until when he wouldn't tell where certain treasure was, he had been slashed in disgust.

Then there was another body, this one stripped naked, and since it was floating face-down Alan could not be sure whether it was man or woman, though he believed that it had been a woman. It was jogging a bit, this body, corking bobbily in

136

the water, as though fishes were working on it from underneath.

Alan made no mention of either of these floating objects. Such sights were supposed to be bad for the spirits of the men.

"A little more to starboard," was all he said.

He drew his sword.

Five minutes later when the little schooner scraped bottom he sprang over the side, his sword held above his head. As he had expected, the water reached only to his chest.

"Come on," he called, and started to wade.

With no hesitation the others followed. They numbered nineteen now, not counting Lennie Harris, who was left with *Lively Lass*. Stumbling, cursing, they staggered up on the beach, where they shook themselves like dogs.

Lem Gray touched his hat to the skipper.

"What's orders now, cap'n, sir?"

"Just follow me, that's all."

With long strides, swishing his sword, Alan started along the beach toward Port Royal.

13

HE HAD never before taken part in an operation on this scale, much less planned one, but he thought he knew what he would do if he was Thomas Meachum. He would land as many men as he could afford, all armed to the teeth, on the beach just outside of the tip end of this peninsula, beyond the reach of those antiquated cannons on Port Henderson Hill. He would cause these men to go shrieking through the whole narrow town, breaking things, brandishing their weapons, killing anybody who got in their way—but not entering any house.

At this, the far end, the eastern end of the town, the end that Alan Waite was approaching now, he would cause them to turn and repeat the process on the way back, at least as far as the warehouse, which he would thereupon attack. He would sack the warehouse, carry the best of the stuff to his boats near the point, and be away from there before a proper counterattack could be organized and brought across or around the bay from the mainland of Kingston.

Would he leave a sort of rearguard at the eastern end of the town to provide against the possibility of a flank attack by some such fast-moving irregular troops as the ones Alan led right now? Alan had asked himself this question. He had decided that it depended largely on whether Meachum could afford the men for such a guard. It depended upon how many, if any, he had lost at his landing and during the course of the rampage through the town. Even more, would depend upon how successful he had been in keeping his followers from looting, from turning aside for rape, from invading the rum shops and getting drunk, always a piratical weakness.

The blaze, Alan believed, must have been caused by an

accident or by sheer exuberance. It could hardly have been a part of the plan. Set so soon, before the attack was more than a few hours old, it would serve to terrify the populace, true, but it might also serve to cut off the transporting of the loot and the retreat of the looters. At the last minute, before taking to the boats—that would be the time to apply a torch.

The end he approached, the east end of town, was not afire. That was one of the reasons why he had picked it.

He only hoped, as he strode toward that cluster of houses, that his own men were following him. They were better than the first lot he'd had assigned to him, but except for Lem Gray he had little faith in them. Yet he didn't dare to turn his head, to see if they were still back there. It would look as though he was nervous; and a leader should never seem nervous.

There was no shot, nor was there any shout, as he entered the town.

The smoke was being blown north, across the bay. The sound of musketry had ceased, and even the crackle of the flames was fainter here, because of the wind, though the flames themselves now were uncomfortably close.

Just at first it might have been a ghost village. Nothing stirred. Yet Meachum's men had lately visited it: that was evident in the splintered jalousies, the bits of cloth and furniture with which the ground was strewn, the doors that had been torn half off their hinges.

That these houses still were occupied seemed likely, but they were occupied by scared men and women who at the sound of footsteps outside only crouched the lower under their mattresses or behind their hastily constructed barricades. Nobody appeared at doorways or at windows. Once, on his right, Alan heard a woman sobbing, an eerie sound. Again, on his left, there was the moan of a man. Nothing else for several minutes.

This made it the more startling when a pirate appeared around the corner of one of the houses. He was very large, and could have been French. He was no member of the Meachum gang anyway, unless he was a recent recruit. His eyes were bloodshot, his mouth slavered. He might have been drunk—either with rum or with lust and the joy of blood-letting—for at the sight of this unexpected, unscheduled column he dropped the miserable tapestries and trinkets he held. He drew, and, bellowing, charged.

Distainfully, Alan Waite leaned aside, but left his leg out for the man to trip over. Alan heard the man's thud, as he himself started on toward the warehouse, the center of town.

"Kill him, somebody," he called over his shoulder. "We can't afford to leave a thing like that in our rear."

He went on.

As he approached the warehouse he saw that he had come too late. The building itself, easily the biggest in town, of three stories, was made of brick and had a corrugated iron roof. It was charred, but except for the main doors not otherwise damaged. This part of town had been burned over, and consisted now of acrid collapsing embers from which smoke rose. The wooden palisade had been charred along the top, and still smouldered, but this had not been done directly by the pirates, who used another means of entry.

The outside wooden gate had been knocked down, and the inner one, of oak, much stronger, the actual door of the warehouse proper, had been smashed to splinters. The ram lay on the ground, discarded once it had served its purpose. It had been carefully prepared for the job it was to do, Tom Meachum, or perhaps his French confederate, his Brother of the Coast, having thought, it would seem, of everything. The ram was relatively short and slim, with spikes for only five swingers on each side, but it was made of native mahogany and so heavy, despite its size, that Alan could not even budge it. Meachum at least, and many or most of the men under him, must have studied that warehouse door many a time, gauging its strength.

That this descent upon Port Royal had in truth been sudden and altogether unexpected—unless it was assumed that the pirates had well-wishers among certain highly-placed parties at Kingston or Spanish Town—was made clear by the brevity of the struggle, the feebleness of the defense. Weakened though it had been by the departure of the convoy, the Royal Navy surely could have sent over at least a handful of men to reinforce the two marines on duty at the gate, while the militia, under energetic leadership, could have thrown at least a token force into the breech.

As it was, the marines must have fought alone. And they seemed to have fought well, if hopelessly. Their muskets, kicked aside now, had been fired. They'd been given no chance to reload these, a long process. Each had his hanger in his right fist. Each had been slashed many times about the head and arms, some of these blows no doubt being struck after the men were down. One body had been hauled to the right, the other to the left, to make way for the men with the battering-ram. Ordinarily the blood, of which there was a great deal would have dried some time ago. Perhaps it was the heat that kept the wounds wet? Here, three or four hours after the time that they had fallen, the two marines still oozed a little, and delighted flies were thick and noisy upon both.

Save for these flies and the wavering tendrils of smoke there was no movement.

141

Alan paused, not in bewilderment but in respect. He almost took off his hat.

Such men as had followed him were not so easily awed. They rushed past him and began to snatch bits of spilled loot from the yard, the doorway, the hall inside, scraps and pieces that the pirates in their haste had dropped—and hadn't bothered to pick up again, perhaps because in the meanwhile the fire had broken out, threatening their passage back to the boats.

There were pitiful pickings—a few small gold coins, squares of linen and silk, short lengths of lace, silver-gilt sword hilts, satin scarves, pearls that had been chipped, glass buttons. Yet such was the greed of the men from *Lively Lass* that only a shower of blows would have brought them to their senses and to a decent respect for their skipper. Even Lemuel Gray was down on hands and knees, scrabbling. They were so scattered, and they moved about so fast, that Alan could not count them with any degree of confidence, but he reckoned that there were about ten here. The rest, he assumed, had ducked into houses along the way to do a little looting, if there was anything left.

He sighed. He went outside to the street.

As though at a signal, as though it had seen him coming, the remaining wall of a nearby house collapsed with a roar, and from it rose swirling smoke and a great wavering, glittering column of sparks. Alan scarcely glanced at it.

Across the way a man rose from some sort of shelter in the very middle of a field of glowing ashes, and leveled a musket at Alan, whom he must have mistaken for a pirate. Alan started to shout, but the explosion gulped the sound of his voice. The ball tore a jagged groove out of the palisade just back of his left shoulder. The man, crouching, ran away.

142

MAROONED

Alan sighed again. He looked to the left, where the fire was the worst, the smoke thickest, the direction of the tip of the town. The Flying Fish was not far away. Though by no means the stronghold that the warehouse had been, the Flying Fish was stout by Port Royal standards, a large, strong, two-story building, the walls of which were partly stucco, partly stone, while the roof was made of corrugated iron. It could have been used as a refuge, a haven, a last stand. It was a natural place for the defenders to rally. Also, Nora might still be there. Nora might need him.

He turned that way.

He went alone. That was a serious mistake, if a human one. He should have kicked his men into compliance with his wishes. But he was so disgusted with them that he didn't have the stomach to heap reproaches upon them.

Coughing, squinting, able to see very little he stepped around four bodies on his way to the Flying Fish. He paused only long enough each time to make sure that it really *was* a body, that no life was left. Two of them had been women. They were nude.

The most celebrated whorehouse in Her Majesty's West Indies had indeed escaped destruction, though it had been mauled and scorched. The door stood open, the walls were blackened, the rattan windowshades torn out, but there was no sign of present occupancy.

His sword drawn, Alan edged in.

The taproom was curiously quiet, as it was desolate. Its magnificent chandeliers had been taken from their hooks and hauled away, though spilled glass prisms, too small to be picked up, lay here and there upon a floor that had been stripped of its rugs. The floor now was strewn with splotches

143

of spittle, chunks of broken bottles, scraps of hangings that no longer decorated the walls.

The tapsters' counter, sometimes called the bar, had of course been swept clear of jacks and mugs and bottles and glasses. In addition, every keg behind it had been rolled away, excepting one, which had been broached—apparently with an ax—right in the middle of the tavern floor, so that its staves jutted this way and that like jackstraws, while the odor of rum filled the air. Alan, however, smelled no blood.

He hoped that the girls had got away in time. Poor twittering, glittering little sluts! He had often cursed them, but he could feel sorry for them now. Scattered, frantic, when caught they would not be carried off, for that was against the practices of the Brotherhood of the Coast. But each, then, would be subjected to a lineup, even if this was right in the midst of the battle, after which her throat would be cut or her back broken so that she couldn't scream any longer.

Alan passed into what had been his own private office behind the bar, at the foot of the stairway, the place where he had been wont to interview prospective customers and to take their fees. It looked much as it had before. It wasn't worth loitering over.

Ahead of him, then, was what had been grandiosely called the Way to Heaven, minus its rich carpeting now. On his left was the kitchen, but he didn't go in there. On his right was a little door that led to an alley, a door through which any customer who had waxed obstreperous in the sacred purlieus above might be expertly thrust—thus saving the scandal of dragging him through the taproom itself, a process that might have depressed the customers. Alan was glad to see that the door stood open. That suggested that the girls might have escaped. He would never take them for another walk in the cool of the late afternoon, but all the same he wished them luck, the poor dears.

He sheathed.

He went up the Way to Heaven, though not with the springy step of most men who had made that climb in the past.

The cribs, the girls' rooms, were in a state of notable disarray. Yet there was nothing in any of them to speak of slaughter.

And would any invader, howsoever Visigothic, howsoever Vandalian, have dared to approach without permission the door of the fine front room that housed Madame?

Alan Waite himself held his breath as he did so.

She had always insisted that he knock before entering. He knocked now.

"Come in."

It was not the voice of Nora Lofts. It was the voice of Harry Swartout.

The acting governor was clad as Alan had seen him in his private home in Kingston—that is, in a scarlet dress uniform, with all his medals and orders, and his epaulettes. Sartorially he was unruffled, a very model, in the midst of this burning ravaged town. It was not so with his emotions. His face was almost as dark a red as his coat, and purple veins throbbed at the temples, while the eyes snapped in fury.

He was standing, and on the bed table at his left lay a pistol. The striker was cocked.

Nora Lofts wore only a shift, no stays, no slippers. Her hair was down her back. She was on the bed, but she was not being seductive. For an instant there was a flicker of hope in her eyes when she saw Alan, but immediately, all fear, she returned her gaze to Colonel Swartout.

It was the first time that Alan had ever seen her look frightened, as it was the first time he ever had seen Swartout at the Flying Fish.

Obviously Alan had interrupted a scene.

"What in hell are *you* doing here? How'd you stay alive?"

Alan bowed. Since he had learned it, he had come to realize when a convenient gesture for concealing feelings the bow could be. When in doubt, clap your hat over your heart and bend from the waist. It gave you whole instants for thought.

"Exactly what Tom Meachum said to me last time I saw him. A coincidence, eh? I seem to be fond of rising from the grave."

"Damn it, Waite, let's have no more of this prattle! How'd you get here?"

"I walked."

"Oh. You walked, eh?"

He swiveled his eyes toward the woman. She did not actually cringe—she was too proud for that—but she answered his stare as though fascinated, as a rabbit might sit transfixed with fright before a snake. She didn't stir. She might have been paralyzed.

For undoubtedly there was murder in the air.

"Well, you aren't the person I was expecting," the colonel went on, "but that needn't matter now. When you walked, then, Waite, you walked into the bedroom of a woman who was born a thief and refused to be lifted from out of that profession. Damn it, d'ye know I saved this bitch from the gallows? D'ye know that, Waite?"

Alan said nothing.

"And what does she do, Waite? Why, aside from letting

you screw her every time you get a chance she proceeds to cheat me systematically out of my earnings. Aye. It's been going on for months. Did you know that, Waite?"

Still Alan did not speak.

"And d'ye know what such behavior merits? Why, it merits this."

He picked up the pistol and pointed it at Nora and fired.

It was done so quickly that Alan Waite didn't get a chance to gasp, to blink. Alan had not even had a flash of fright that it was *he* who was about to be shot. There was a terrific explosion. Nora Lofts was shrouded in smoke; and then the smoke cleared, and Nora was dead.

The colonel had used his left hand, but at that distance—scarcely a foot—he could not have missed.

Nora Lofts seemed to spring away from the shock, as though she had shoved herself with her own feet. Her head snapped back. That head, as well as an arm and a shoulder, then a breast, went over the far side of the bed, while dull dark blood widened on her shift.

She started to slip off the bed, very quietly as though, conscious still, she was trying to see how long she could make the trick last.

The smoke broke into low twisting rivulets and lost itself near the floor.

Swartout glared at Alan.

"Well, what're you going to do about it?"

He threw the pistol at Alan.

Alan dodged, but as he dodged he drew.

"I am going to kill you," he answered.

In the fencing school they teach a man that he must never be personal about the business, never emotional. He can't afford that. So great a degree of concentration, mental and physical alike, is required in the sport, the masters say, that exultation, anger, fear, timorousness, even a mild degree of annoyance, inevitably become handicaps. Unless the man you face is not really a man but only a weapon, they tell you, you cannot do your best fencing. The notion of "inspired" swordsmanship is nonsense.

Alan Waite would have fought anyway. He probably would have been given no choice. And he couldn't crush from himself, even for a little while, his hatred of Harry Swartout. His only hope was that the acting governor was shaken by a hatred even more violent, even more distracting, that he was, in effect, what he certainly seemed to be—insane. This might narrow the odds.

Could it be that they were wrong in the fencing schools? Or was Harry Swartout a phenomenon? He might have been mad, yes, but his sword wasn't. His sword was exceedingly, perilously sane.

His draw was like a flash of light, and as he dropped into guard position, perfectly poised, it was patent that he knew only one thing in this whole wide world—the annihilation of Alan Waite.

At first he did not stir, only stood waiting, hoping that Alan would attack.

This, Alan, bluntly, was afraid to do. He beat the colonel's blade a little, first on one side, then on the other, flea-bites to which the colonel paid no heed; but Alan was afraid to lunge. He knew from experience the lightning speed of the colonel's riposte. There were no buttons on the points now.

At last Swartout, scowling absently, began to cat-step forward. He made no wild feints or counters. He did not move his blade in any way, only his feet.

MAROONED

Alan retreated.

The mortal remains of Nora Lofts slipped off the bed entirely, and thumped to the floor. It did not seem possible that so willowy a woman could make so great a noise.

Swartout came in a little farther, Alan retreating.

They eyed one another for a long moment.

Suddenly the colonel raised his blade to the high line, his point directed at Alan's eyes, while he straightened his arm the way the Italians sometimes did. Alan refused to follow, or to be daunted by the point. Yet Alan still was afraid to attack.

The colonel dropped his guard again, and edged in.

Alan's left foot met the wall behind him. He could retreat no farther.

He lunged.

He never knew how it happened. The sword was snicked out of his hand as neatly as if it had been a quill pen snatched away from behind. Swartout stepped back, his guard high. Alan's sword struck the ceiling, then fell ten or twelve feet away. It made a great clatter.

Alan could not possibly have reached it.

The colonel smiled, but there were spikes in the smile.

The colonel, his point now directed at Alan's breast, his arm straight, crept in.

"Now," he whispered.

The door flew open.

"What the Devil's going on here?" demanded Thomas Meachum.

14

NEITHER Meachum nor Swartout seemed amazed, and an astounded Alan Waite deduced or sensed instantly that this meeting had been arranged, that it was a rendezvous. These two could hardly have met at any previous time, yet each had been expecting the other. They had made the engagement through an intermediary. It was what the acting governor had been waiting for. It was why he had hidden himself here.

They presented a striking contrast. Each was a large man, each disagreeable, forceful, plain-spoken, unscrupulous. Yet though there were some pirates with a fondness for finery—Alan knew a few who at a share-out would accept all sorts of sacrifices if they could but get a pair of red-heeled shoes, a pair of dove-colored stockings, a well-starched stock—Thomas Meachum was not one of these. Facing the dapper colonel, Meachum, always shaggy, sloppy, today suggested something that had been dragged across a cinder pit at the tail of a horse.

He stank. He fairly reeked. His hat had been lost, and his hair—it was his own hair, greasy black stuff—fell in a tangled mass to the shoulders of a much-ripped coat. One sleeve of that coat had been torn entirely off. His face had been blackened by smoke, and his beard singed. His dark-blue eyes gleamed with a vulperine brightness. The only clean thing about him was a fine cordovan leather swordbelt, behind which were thrust two daggers and a large brass-barreled pistol. Gunpowder stippled the muzzle of that pistol, from which Alan inferred that it had recently been fired.

"We were fighting," Swartout said coldly. "Any objections?"

MAROONED

The pirate king's glance flicked across the body of Nora Lofts.

"I thought it was understood that you'd be alone?"

"I thought it was understood that your men would stay away from this house?"

"I can't see to everything, at a time like this. You were lucky they didn't come into this room."

"Perhaps *they* were lucky." The colonel shrugged. "Well, I had an account to settle with the regular occupant here, and this seemed as good a time as any to do it."

"I see."

"But I was interrupted."

Swartout nodded to Alan Waite. Meachum turned.

"You again! How do you keep coming back alive?"

Alan grinned.

"It is odd, isn't it? The lieutenant-governor and I were just talking about that."

"And the lieutenant-governor and *me* had a bargain that you was to stay dead this time."

He glared at Swartout.

"Something slipped up," the colonel said. "I might have known it. The Navy never does anything right. But never mind. I was about to finish the job myself, when you came in. So, if you'll step aside . . ."

He raised the point of his sword.

But Meachum shook an impatient head.

"That can wait. We've got our business to settle first. If I don't get out of here soon I may not be able to reach the boats."

"What of it? They wouldn't go without you."

"Oh, wouldn't they just! They'd jump at the chance! It would mean more for every one of them in the share-out. And

that's what I want to talk to you about. That share-out won't
be anywhere near as big as I'd been led to expect."

"A scavenger," Colonel Swartout pointed out, "custom-
arily takes what he can get."

"Yes, we're scavengers. But even a scavenger's got a right
to expect a man to live up to his contract. I came here, didn't
I, the way we'd agreed? And I didn't bring anybody with me."

"All right. Did you bring a tenth share?"

"No. Why should I, when that warehouse had been looted
first, before we ever got there?"

"What the Devil do you mean, sir?"

"You know damned well what I mean! You've been governor and treasurer and practically everything else of this island
for more than a year now, and you could do just about anything you wanted to with the goods in that place—until the
royal commissions arrive from Home and the real governor
starts looking into your official affairs."

"See here, are you implying that I stole something?"

"I aint implying it, I'm saying it."

For the moment they had forgotten Alan Waite, yet Alan
didn't dare dash for the open door. Swartout, his sword bare
in his hand, could easily have cut him down before he got
there.

"Damn you! You'll apologize for that!"

"Damn you, I won't do any such thing. When I make a
deal with a man who's an officer in the English Army I got
a right to expect some sort of honesty."

"You're a fine one to be talking about honesty!"

"I never pretended to be anything but a pirate. But you—
Well, all we got there was some silks and woolens and the like
of that. Clayed sugar, rum and wine, brazilletto and man-
chineel.

152

MAROONED

"What d'ye expect, diamond-studded gold peacocks?"

"Well, what ever happened to them chests of Spanish eight-pieces that everybody knows was there? And the caskets of Panama pearls? And the candelabras and chalices and so forth that they took off that Portugee ship, *Nuestra Señora de la Concepción*? Where are they?"

"Damn you, draw!"

"You just wanted us to make a raid so's you could cover up your own stealing. Well, we don't work that way. *We* steal *openly*."

"I said, *draw!*"

"Sure."

Very cautiously Alan edged toward his sword, which lay on the floor near the foot of the bed. He would not have much time. Harry Swartout would skewer this clumsy pirate in a matter of seconds, he was sure.

Meachum charged, bellowing like a bull, his blade high. He was wide open. He should have been run through right then and there, at almost any point Swartout cared to choose. But Swartout, a mite startled by such ferocity, stepped backward, and he must have slipped on something.

That was the only possible explanation—that he had stepped on something Alan didn't see. He teetered, screeching, trying to regain his balance. He threw up both arms. And the pirate's blade got him squarely on the top of the head.

It sounded like splitting a melon.

Harry Swartout stood still for an instant, his mouth open, his eyes squints of astonishment. Blood began to stream down his forehead, down his temples and cheeks. The blood came eagerly, rapidly.

Swartout blinked. He gulped. Then his knees gave, and he pitched forward upon his face.

MAROONED

If he had fallen backward he would have fallen against Alan Waite.

On the assumption that Swartout would advance and Meachum retreat, Alan had started to move not behind Meachum for the open door but behind Swartout for the foot of the bed. The outcome, so swiftly arrived at, the reverse of what he'd expected, caught him entirely unprepared.

"So?" said Tom Meachum. "And now you."

He raised his sword again.

Alan, facing the door now, dropped his lower jaw, popped his eyes.

"My God!" he whispered.

Here was one of the oldest tricks in the repertoire of the rascal. That Meachum responded to it could be accounted for only by his stupidity, his mental slowness.

He turned his head to look at the doorway.

Alan sprang to the sword, lifted it, and in an instant was at guard position.

"Ye dog!"

The pirate knew nothing about defense, and could only attack. He went in high, as he had done with Harry Swartout. In his simple mind an assault that had worked once would work again.

Alan did not retreat. He only bent his knees and straightened his sword arm, the point tipped up.

Meachum's edge swished empty air. And Meachum himself, by the very force of his charge, fairly thrust his own throat upon Alan's point, which drove through it, coming out a full three inches at the back of the neck.

It almost snapped Alan's blade when Tom Meachum crashed to the floor.

MAROONED

There was no need to examine Tom Meachum. No man could live after taking one like that.

Panting, Alan looked around.

Nora Lofts lay on the far side of the bed, on her back, one arm outflung, the palm up. Her hair, that soft reddish-brown hair that Alan had loved to caress, was not in disarray. The green eyes were open, but they showed no more fear, only serenity. Except for the gaping black hole in the very middle of her breast, she might have been asleep.

But no. There was something wrong.

Alan went to her, knelt by her side. He studied her.

The earing! She wore only one earing, a pear-shaped emerald pendant, one of a pair that Harry Swartout himself had given her. That was not like Nora, a very neat woman.

Could it have been thrown off when Nora was flung to the bed, just before Alan entered?

He went to Swartout. Yes, there a few inches from one of the colonel's feet lay the other earing. Beyond all doubt that was what the colonel had stepped on, it was what cost him his life.

Alan took the thing back to Nora, and fastened it on the right ear, where it belonged. She had always like to have things tidy. He found a cloak for her, and wrapped her in this, preparing to carry her outside.

For it would never do to leave the body here. If Meachum's friends came looking for him there was no telling how they might violate it.

She was unexpectedly light, and lay like a broken doll in his arms. Perhaps her backbone had been severed? Poor child! Like Alan, she had come from nowhere, and like him she'd had to fight for whatever she got—fight, that is, in her own way. That she had lost at last was not to be won-

155

dered at. Indeed, it was just as well, for old age, assuredly, would not have been kind to Nora Lofts.

Alan carried her downstairs, and he took her out by the back door, as was only fitting.

He scooped a shallow grave for her in what had seemingly been somebody's vegetable garden, covered now with ashes and chunks of charred wood. She had not been a pretentious woman. She would not have wanted a tombstone.

He knelt there a moment, and though he was no praying man he did weep.

When he got to his feet and looked again toward the bay he saw that the skimmers were nearing shore. But there was no more shooting, for the pirates on the outside beach were already shoving off, without their king. Most of the fires were out, and those that remained were burning only stodgily.

Port Royal had been saved—what was left of it.

Governor Handasyde—the commissions had arrived at last—was a handsome man, a man of befitting gravity. His eulogy was a masterpiece, despite the fact that almost everybody knew it to be a face-saving lie, uttered for the purpose of maintaining the good name of the colony.

True, there were those who, from time to time, had hinted of irregular or at least unusual financial practices on the part of the deceased, he conceded, but the clerks had triumphantly disproved this when they accounted for every penny of the money at the disposal of the deceased in his official capacity.

"We need no longer think of him as a harsh man, a hard-driving man. We should think now of the reasons why we have just given him a military funeral with all the honors of war. He died a hero, fighting the enemies of his country, and fighting them singlehandedly."

MAROONED

Helena pressed Alan's hand. In a few days—it had been thought proper to allow a decent interval to pass—they would be standing side by side in this very church, at the altar. Alan's commission as major of militia had been confirmed, but his duties would not often take him away from the vast Huntington plantation, where he had been made chief overseer.

"Why do you let him say that," she whispered, "when you know better?"

"Sh-sh! What harm will it do?"

"But he's not a hero at all! He was a thief!"

"Sh-sh! He did die fighting. And he was a military man. He would have loved this. Why not give him credit for having killed Tom Meachum? It makes everybody happier that way."

She squeezed his hand again. She was very proud of him.

"It has been written that he who lives by the sword shall perish by the sword, and the deceased, I think, would gladly have subscribed to that," Governor Handasyde went on. "It was his free choice. And if it projected him into his grave, as we have just seen, at least it enabled him to be borne there covered with such a robe of glory as might befit any officer and any English gentleman."

"Amen," cried the minister.

And they all said "Amen."